AF485216

Death: In the Key of C

A Jake Rivers Adventure

#14

Books by Joe Mannherz

All For Nothing
Home Grown
Stage Fly
'Twas the Night
Rescued
Forfeit
Undeterred
Rivers Run
While You Weren't Looking
None the Wiser
The Prodigal Son
Said She, Said He
The Black Widower
Death: In the Key of C

The Tale of Jonathan T. Bookworm
The Account of Hercules A. Gnawer

Table of Contents

Prologue

Chapter 1 . . . . Sounds Good to Me

Chapter 2 . . . . Anton Rinaldi

Chapter 3 . . . . Melissa Crane

Chapter 4 . . . . Doctor Eli Cassilly

Chapter 5 . . . . Jonah Pyke

Chapter 6 . . . . Music Therapy 101

Chapter 7 . . . . The Rhapsody in C

Chapter 8 . . . . D.S. al Coda

Chapter 9 . . . . The Sign

Chapter 10 . . . Accelerando

Chapter 11 . . . Crescendo

Chapter 12 . . . Repeat

Chapter 13 . . . 1st Ending

Chapter 14 . . . Requiem for a Pianist

Chapter 15 . . . On the Homefront

Chapter 16 . . . ppp (pianississimo)

Chapter 17 . . . Rubato

Chapter 18 . . . Decelerando Decrescendo

Chapter 19 . . . Coda

Reprise

Epilogue

Dedication

For all those I have shared
the stage with:
Here's to breaking more
legs together.

Adagio
N. 33.
Quartetto VI.
Violino
Viola
Violoncello
Adagio
cresc. for
cresc. for
cresc. for
cresc.
cresc.
cresc.
p
pia.
pia.
for.
for.

PROLOGUE

Music was her life.
She would cease to exist without it.
Little did she know that her life
would cease because of it.

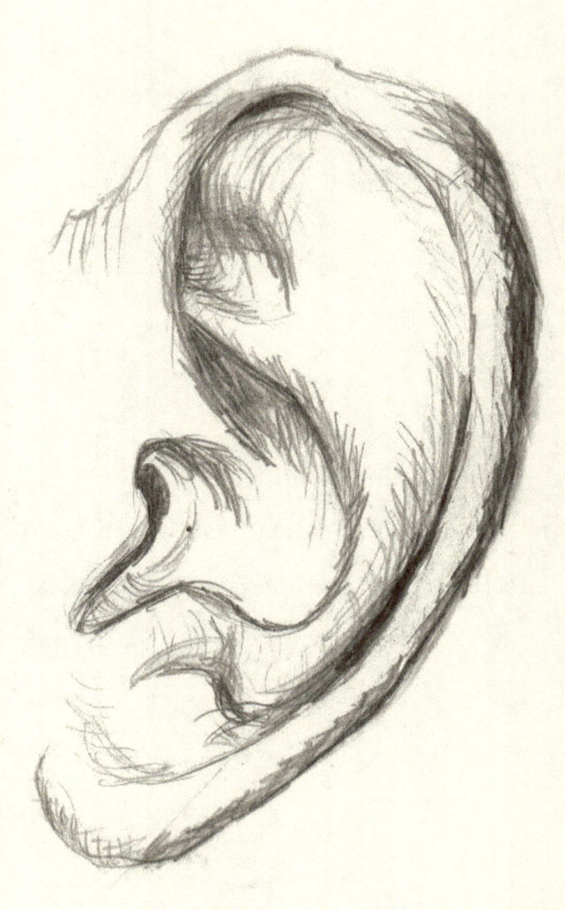

CHAPTER 1

Sounds Good to Me

[Beep}

Apprehensive and anxious didn't come anywhere close to describing the way she was feeling at the moment. Truth be told, she didn't want to be here in the first place. But coercion is a strong motivator. Well, maybe coercion was too strong of a word to describe her niece's persistent insistence. She knew her niece had her best interest at heart, that's why she relented. That's why she was sitting here imposing death grips on the arms of her chair.

She could think of 100 different places she could be at this very moment, and this wasn't one of them. The one place she should be, but wasn't, if it could talk, would give her 88 reasons to remain exactly where she was; and she knew it. Resignation to that knowledge reverberated in her very bones, but unfortunately, that's not where she needed the help. The bones she needed help with lay in a completely different location in her body.

[Beep]

Sequestered and isolated as she was, in a soundproof room, with state-of-the-art noise cancelling headphones covering both her ears while she stared at the blank white wall some six feet away from where her perspiring and trembling body resided, was unnerving. She felt like she was awaiting Houston's space center's countdown, to be eventually blasted off the face of the earth into orbit, to go, God-only-knows where, in space. And not knowing where, or even why she was going, gave her pause to consider how the astronauts must feel each time they're strapped into the seats of their projectiles rocket, pre-launch.

Anticipation, in either case, was the proverbial nemesis. Anticipation of the unknown. And the result of which could make or break everyone's career, from astronaut to musician; especially hers. And that's what she was afraid of. One would think the monumental possibility of a positive outcome to her current endeavors would outweigh the fear of failure, which itself was overwhelming to begin with, but somehow, it didn't. Somehow, the prospect of failure was mind numbing and led to her current state of catatonia. A state she rarely found her body residing in, taking into account her life's vocation. But alas, even after a deep dive into underlying self-awareness, five intentionally slow and shallow biorhythmic inspirations, as well as Hindu inspired meditative, contemplative mind exercises to reduce her anxiety, it took every bit of self-control to keep her from climbing the walls.

[Beep]

She knew what to expect. It had been explained to her very thoroughly prior to her entering her current location. But even that was poor consolation to her ever-mounting paranoia. Maybe some situations were best left alone. Maybe this was the way God intended her to be, and who was she to interfere with the Almighty's plan for her.

"But, if this could help, wouldn't it be worth it?" she thought, in order to distract herself away from debating with the creator and questioning the fates. All of which, she was quite aware, was an 'experiment-in-futility.' But she knew, from all the specialists she had seen who had given her the same results via countless tests she had taken, that her current situation was permanent and very likely was going to get worse. 'Staying-the-course' and minding the 'status quo' was therefore not an option. What else could she do? That's why she let her niece 'persuade' her to undertake her current 'plan-of-action.' No matter how unnerved and anxious she was currently, she realized the wisdom and necessity of her recent decision.

[Beep]

"What was that?" she asked herself, after the silent world she had been existing in for the last several minutes: changed. She hesitated, trying desperately to overcome her current catatonic state, to react to what she possibly could have mistaken as a sound. She wasn't sure. She wasn't sure if the interruption of silence was real or just a figment of her imagination. Her reaction, however, didn't go unnoticed.

[Beep]

There it was again. This time, she was sure. This time, she was certain. So, she raised her right hand as previously instructed.

She turned around in her chair, an action directly against 'previous instructions,' to glare through the wall of glass, which separated her from her examiner, with the look of anticipation on her face. A look fashioned in the hope of getting a reaction of approval, as a child in school would, wanting confirmation from her teacher for supplying the correct answer to the math problem.

All she received from the audiologist was a signal to turn back around in her chair and continue the testing. She reluctantly but hopefully did so in anticipation of sounds not yet heard.

After more than an hour of raising and lowering respective hands to perceived sounds, the door to her makeshift acoustic space capsule opened and the Doctor of audiology beckoned her forth into a now, relatively unknown, mysterious, but hope filled new world.

"So, how did it go?" asked Claire Adams of her aunt, as she greeted her with a warm embrace when she re-entered the reception area.

"Didn't hurt a bit," lied Marjorie Cunningham to her niece. *"Not physically, anyway,"* she then admitted to herself.

"Told 'ja," claimed Claire, in a 'I-told-you-so' retort, accompanied by apropos facial expressions and body language.

Marjorie had to admit to herself that her niece was right, but she wasn't going to let her get away with that attitude.

"OK, so that makes once in your life. Don't get used to it," Marjorie exclaimed, while giving her niece a reprimanding poke in the ribs, and an affectionate smile to match.

Claire, a precocious 23-year-old, admired her aunt beyond words. Jealous of her beauty, and envious of her talent, she couldn't love her mother's sister anymore if she tried. Marjorie had raised Claire from a young age, after her only sister, a single mother, had passed away from ovarian cancer, leaving Claire in her charge. The two of them couldn't have been closer, even if Marjorie was Claire's biological mother, which, of course, she wasn't.

'Thicker-than-thieves' would have been the old-fashioned term to describe the pair. They went everywhere together, did everything together, and, on occasion, even wore each other's clothes. Is it any wonder then that Marjorie Cunningham would entrust to her closest confidant, her niece, her deepest and most disconcerting secret; that she, not as her aunt, but as one of the world's most renowned classical pianists, was losing her hearing.

As with all things that degrade with time, Marjorie was unaware of the infinitesimal diminishment of her hearing, day after day, until the accumulated syndromic effect of prolonged environmental 'orchestral' noise, combined with the over use of Furosemide (Lasix) and Naproxen, used to relieve swelling and pain in her hands and wrists, as well as assist managing her slightly elevated blood pressure, produced deleterious effects (Ototoxicity) within her inner ear bone structure as well as the cilia of her cochlea. Getting into arguments concerning performance parameters, i.e., concerning tempo, meter or even style was commonplace between pianists and conductors, performers and composers. But when she started missing cues, verbally spoken by those same conductors/composers, she had to start making excuses for what she didn't hear. And, at that time, she didn't know why.

The same could be said about miscommunication dilemma's using the phone, poor perception of background speech unrecognizable amidst crowd cacophony, or the recent involuntary need to increase the volume on her television or car radio. And most devastating of all was her encroaching inability to appreciate the full resonance of her instrument, the piano. Initially she blamed the malady on inept piano tuners, poor room acoustics, inferior pianos, etc. You name it; she blamed it.

Not until her niece's ongoing perceptive observations concerning same were brought to Marjorie's attention, and at times, forcibly so, did Marjorie take Claire's message to heart and acknowledge her unfortunate shortcomings. Once she did so, Claire was able to 'convince' her favorite aunt that she needed to seek professional help. Reluctantly, Marjorie acquiesced.

The doctors, and there were many who examined her, didn't paint Marjorie's continued hearing future with bright colors. They could slow down the progression of her hearing loss but could not stop it. They also claimed that in the interim, they could make her hearing better by way of inner canal hearing aids.

And here she was, sitting with her niece in the reception area of the audiologist, both disheartened and anxious, awaiting the outcome of her tests and the prognostication of her hearing's future.

"Why the long face? Queried the bartender of the horse that just cantered into his saloon," asked Claire of Marjorie, breaking the silence that existed not only between them but everywhere else in the room. The appropriate joke hung in the air, unanswered, because the latter of the two women looked like her dog just died.

"Oh, come on," chastised Claire, "it's not that bad. You're getting a chance to hear again. Don't you want that?"

"Yeah, but for how long?" was Marjorie's morose reply.

Claire could empathize completely with what her aunt was going through, but she was damned if she was going to sit here and let her aunt feel sorry for herself.

"What would Beethoven think of this?" Claire berated.

"What?" exclaimed Marjorie, after being taken off guard.

"Beethoven! You've heard of Beethoven? No pun intended. What do you think Beethoven would do or say, if for just one moment, science could give him back his hearing? Do you think he would be sitting here bemoaning the future? I bet you not! I'd bet you he'd be running to the nearest piano to play all the music he composed and never got the chance to hear while alive. And look at you! You're being given the chance to enjoy all the music you can play for as long as you can play it, or hear it, and you're sitting here looking like you're waiting for your number to be called for the guillotine. I don't get it!"

Claire, almost heartbroken over what she had just said, knew that she had hit the right 'chord' as she watched the tears cascade down her aunt's cheeks in response to her beratement.

When words won't do, actions must suffice. Marjorie, in acknowledging the wisdom of Claire's statement but unable to thank her sufficiently with words, just bridged the gap between where they were seated and enveloped her niece in an embrace.

This touching scene, appreciated by all the clinic's clientele, was broken, when the audiologist, in person, called the two women back into her office.

"Our computer has all your test results and is, even as we speak, designing your remote module, which will be incorporated into your smart phone, with your required parameters, and should be ready within the week. From there you can adjust just about all audible frequencies, volumes, and tones that are humanly possible. It'll even be Bluetooth compatible with any device so equipped. You'll even be able to pick up radio and television stations if you so desire. This will time perfectly with the construction of your personalized inner ear aids taken from the molds we made just this morning. As soon as all that's completed, I'll give you a call and you can come in and we'll show you how to apply them and how they work."

Claire nodded toward the audiologist as a sign of her complete understanding. Not so true in Marjorie's case. She still had that 'dead dog' look in her eyes as she stared past the audiologist while absentmindedly touching her ears.

"Now what?" exclaimed a bewildered Claire.

"But everybody will be able to see them," bemoaned Marjorie.

Claire remained still for a few seconds because she couldn't believe her own ears. Here sat her aunt, one of the world's greatest living pianists, with the possibility of hearing as close to normal as modern science good bring her, looming within reach, and she was going to let her vanity get in the way?

"Beethoven!" reminded Claire.

This comment appeared to bring Marjorie out of her self-imposed trance, although the utterance and its meaning were lost on the audiologist herself.

"Don't you remember? They told you that the only part of the apparatus that protrudes from the ear is the miniscule quarter inch antenna. You could start wearing your hair longer again, like you did five years ago. That way, the only people in the world that will know that you're wearing hearing aids are you, me, and the audiologist. And my lips are sealed," claimed Claire, as she drew her fingers across her lips, metaphorically sealing them.

This statement of finality seemed to have lightened the air in the room sufficiently enough, to allow the two women to bid the audiologist a cordial goodbye and make their way out of her office to attend a preplanned luncheon after this very occasion.

Meanwhile, after bidding the women goodbye in return, and subsequently closing the door, the audiologist picked up her desk phone and placed a call to an all too familiar number.

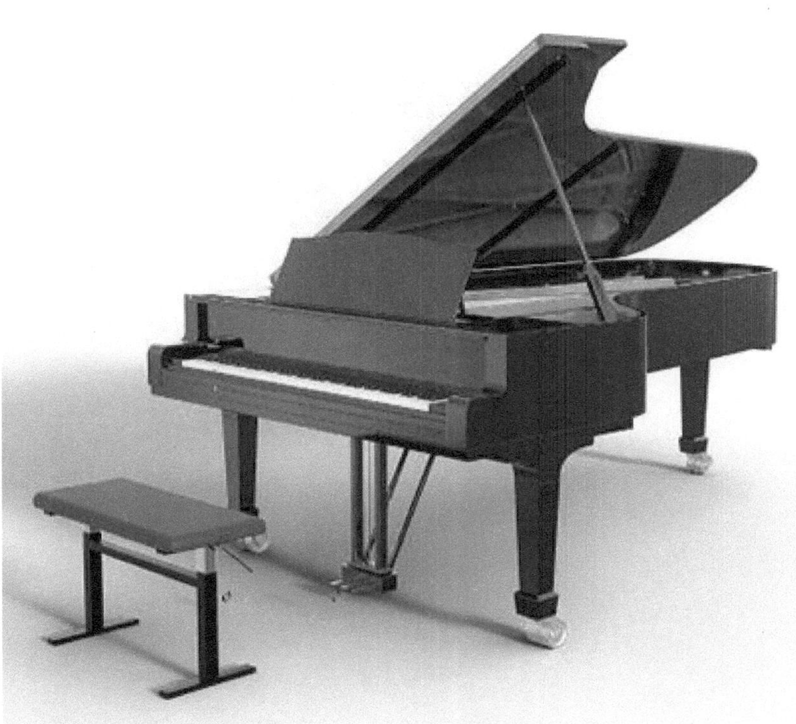

Chapter 2

Anton Rinaldi

Graduate of the Peabody Conservatory and the Juilliard School. Composer and current conductor of the Baltimore Symphony Orchestra based out of the Joseph Meyerhoff Symphony Hall in downtown Baltimore.

-- Five years ago –

Time: 10 am

Location: Lower rehearsal hall, located in the basement of the Meyerhoff Symphony Hall, three weeks prior to its scheduled concert of Tchaikovsky's Piano Concerto #1 in B-flat minor, Opus 23.

Out of breath, slightly red faced and looking perturbed, Anton slowly lowered his arms and ceased to conduct the more than 100 musicians assembled in front of him, only to glare at the pianist seated to his left.

The orchestra members, now quite familiar with this gesture, slowly abandoned the playing of their instruments, in a cascading effect, that sounded remarkably like an old wind-up Victrola running out of spring power.

"You're playing slightly ahead of my stick, again. And getting louder, again," remarked Anton, in an authoritarian, reprimanding manner.

"I thought we had agreed on the tempo throughout this section, as well as maintaining the pianissimo?" he inquired.

"We may have discussed this, but I don't remember coming to any definite conclusions about velocity and volume. Tchaikovsky's own handwritten, marginal inscriptions indicate that he wanted to begin accelerating at measure 14 and crescendo into the next movement. I ascribe to this treatment of the score, it makes sense," stated Marjorie, while crossing her arms on her chest in a defiant gesture.

"I don't care what you 'ascribe' too, or what you think Tchaikovsky may or might have suggested as a treatment for this section of music. It's been played successfully at my tempo for generations, everywhere, and I don't see the necessity or the need to change time tested, approved protocol now," insisted Anton.

"But changing time tested, approved protocol isn't necessarily bad. If you would just . . ."

"Everybody take five," instructed Anton to the orchestra, cutting off Marjorie midsentence, before, what he assumed, would be more debating over the score's treatment that would occur, in public.

"Not you!" he insisted of Marjorie, wanting to make sure she didn't follow her fellow musicians to the breakroom.

The orchestra members were more than happy to accede to Anton's request, because they didn't want to be witness, again, to the pairs 'differences-of-opinion,' again. They sheepishly filed out of the rehearsal hall, with many giving the two remaining musical antagonists an empathetic back glance.

Once they were alone, Anton took the opportunity to come down off his dais and advance on Marjorie, asking,

"What are you doing?"

"I thought by now that would be obvious," she responded.

"The only thing obvious about this is that you're holding up rehearsals and wasting precious time. Time, that at present, is turning into a rare commodity."

"I, and _it_ wouldn't be, if you would be less rigid in your approach to conducting this gorgeous piece of music and let it speak to you, as it is speaking to me," she replied by means of explanation.

"The only thing I hear it saying, is that if we don't finish rehearsing this piece of music by the time the curtain goes up three weeks from now, and we're not ready, when the less than credible reviews come out, and the symphony's Board of Trustees starts losing money because the unfavorable word on the street is causing attendance to plummet, both you and I are going to be looking for work, elsewhere."

Money. Why did artistry always seem to suffer in the face of monetary parameters. Did he even stop to consider, that if the already acknowledged masterpiece could be lifted off its pedestal and elevated to new heights; that its new acclaim could usher in a resurgence of interest, as well as monetary 'contributions' via greater attendance by the public. Apparently not, was the conclusion Marjorie came away with after their brief 'exchange.' Sensing that further discussion on the topic would be futile, Marjorie rested her hands on the piano's headboard as a passive sign of resignation. Anton also took the gesture as such, as he turned and retook the podium just as the members of the orchestra began strolling into the hall.

Several minutes of unsettling silence passed in the room, not only between the two 'combatants,' but the orchestra members as well. As the latter took their seats, mental curiosity as to the 'yet-to-be-stated' outcome of the recent parlay started to mount.

Just before the members had a chance to take up their instruments, or Maestro Rinaldi began speaking, Marjorie began to play --- alone. She started playing the symphony several pages prior to their recently 'disagreed upon' section. With her eyes closed, relying on memory and feeling alone, she masterfully proceeded to engulf the room with the music of Tchaikovsky. Bridging the gap over the disputed measures, Marjorie relied upon her instincts. And with the ethereal blessings of the composer behind her, she began to modulate measure by measure, advancing both tempo and volume, until her intended interpretation of the passage flowed seamlessly into the resounding melody that the composer had intended, and that his audiences revere even to this day. Allowing herself time to complete the phrase, Marjorie maneuvered and eventually stopped at a natural resolution of the musical sentence.

Audible sighs and gasps of air could be heard emanating from the assemblage. These were followed by numerous bows and hands lightly tapping their approval on respective music stands.

Eventually, Marjorie opened her eyes. And to her surprise, she was confronted, not by the stern expression she was expecting from the maestro, but by a smirk of approval.

"Ok," he stated in soft resignation, while picking up his baton. "Just like that from now on, starting at letter 'E.' He then addressed his next comment to the woman seated at the piano:

"Touche;' but just this once."

But it wasn't 'just this once.' Their musically contentious relationship continued in this manner for years thereafter. The orchestra saw this play out as a benefit to them, because the outcome usually meant a better performance all the way around, regardless of the piece of music on which they were collaborating. Marjorie appreciated the debates, and chalked them up as professional, personal and spiritual growth. Anton, however, just considered Marjorie a pain in his ass and someone he could almost do without.

So, it was with great reluctance that he sought out Marjorie Cunningham for his newly penned Rhapsody in C for piano and orchestra. He might have had a contemptuous relationship with her over the years, but, as a performer and musician himself, and someone who was constantly watching his 'bottom line,' he wasn't stupid.

-- 5 weeks ago –

Time: 9 am

Location: Lower rehearsal hall, located in the basement of the Meyerhoff Symphony Hall, three weeks prior to its scheduled premiere of Anton Rinaldi's Rhapsody in the Key of C for piano and orchestra.

Patiently awaiting the arrival of the maestro/composer sat Marjorie Cunningham, the pianist, as well as the rest of the orchestra, biding their time on the proverbial clock.

The Rhapsody, in and of itself as written, was wonderful. Marjorie thought so the moment she laid eyes on it. And her initial impressions of the work were emotionally and professionally verified after her initial 'run-through' of the piece. What it lacked, however, was a soul.

Rhapsodies, generally consisting of one movement, utilize contrasting moods, ideas and themes to move its listeners. Perfect examples of this could be found in Gershwin's Rhapsody in Blue or Rachmaninoff's Variation on a Theme of Paganini. Both exemplified the feeling which embodied improvisational spontaneity.

The Rhapsody in C, his Rhapsody, the work penned by Anton Rinaldi, as written, had potential, but wasn't there yet, according to Marjorie. It lacked the tone, emotion and color needed for the piece to soar. It was there, on paper, but Anton wasn't performing it the way it needed to be played. The multiple themes were present, in ink, but he wasn't letting them breathe or blossom. He was treating them all the same. He was painting his beautifully composed masterpiece with the same undersized paintbrush. Marjorie saw the potential therein but was emotionally, as well as physically constrained from pointing this out, taking into account their sorted past.

As she was contemplating her conflicting emotions, the source of her juxtaposition entered the hall.

Finally, she realized that, as a performer, she had to honor the music, in the only way she knew how, come what may. Besides, what emotional choice did she have? She acquiesced to let the fates decide as she watched Anton Rinaldi stride to the podium and take up his baton.

The rehearsal began in earnest and proceeded a quarter of the way into the piece without a hitch, until the time came for a variant, beckoning for the mood to change, dominated the proceedings. The need to create another 'message' loomed over Anton's creation, and Marjorie 'went-with-the-flow.'

So ingrained and intrenched was she in her interpretation of the music that she didn't realize that she was the only one playing, until the first violinist, the concertmaster of the orchestra, the conductor's first lieutenant, coughed.

Coming to grips with reality, a confused Marjorie, after ceasing to play herself, visually scanned the hall, only to find the collective members of the orchestra smiling in her direction. Her amazement was short lived however, when her gaze finally fell upon the distorted and angry expression of Anton.

"Everybody take five," was all that Anton intoned. With a stare that could freeze water, Anton fixed his unrelenting gaze upon Marjorie, as the members of the orchestra departed as instructed.

"What do you think you're doing?" thundered Anton, hurling the admonishment as hard as he could in Marjorie's direction.

"I'm picking up where Tchaikovsky left off," remarked Marjorie, as a reminder of the past.

Anton didn't need to be reminded. Whenever he was in her presence, he was reminded. But this was his creation, not Tchaikovsky's. It was one thing to interpret a long-deceased master. It was quite another altogether to interfere with the directives of the work's composer, and director, who was standing right in front of you.

Knowing the precise and exact professional situation she was 'standing in,' but in the vain hope of lightening the mood, she replied:

"What can I say, it needed some help."

Unfortunately, that was not the appropriate or adequate response Anton Rinaldi was looking for. In fact, that reply only heightened Anton's animosity towards Marjorie, not to mention elevating his blood pressure, to the point where he decried:

"That's it, you're out. I'm bringing in Melissa Crane."

"Who?" replied a surprised Marjorie.

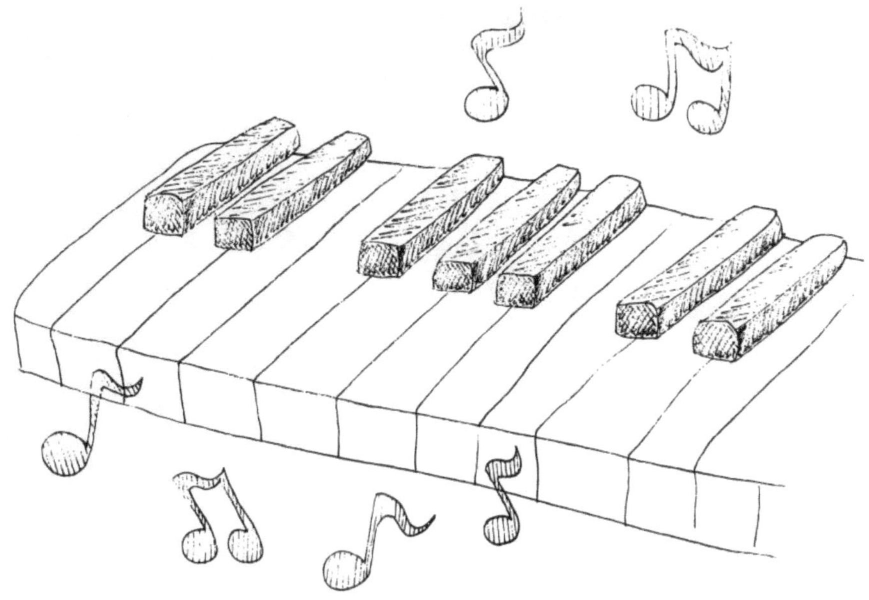

PianoDisc

Chapter 3
Melissa Crane

Pianist. Graduate of the Curtis Institute and the Eastman School of Music. Classmate of Marjorie Cunningham.

It felt as if the rivalry started the first time they ever met. Envious of each other's looks, as well as talent, they vied for the attention and approval of their pedagogue on the first day of class, and it hasn't stopped since.

Playing one-upmanship for as long as they could remember, each tried to outdo the other in grades, being the first to master a given concerto, to who could win the most prestigious piano recital competitions in any given year. The latter, more than not, were claimed by Marjorie.

Although both women were technically perfect, i.e., every note of the composition struck, every keystroke in time and with the predetermined volume. Melissa played the piano perfectly, but Marjorie made it sing. Marjorie's piano talked to its audience in a way that the uplifting communication between her keyboard and each individual listener was private and personal. This was the difference between a piano player and a pianist. And this was the inherent detail that separated the two women then, and now.

Major orchestras and renowned composers sought out Marjorie Cunningham for just this reason. They wanted their music to come alive, and Marjorie fulfilled their wishes. Needless to say, Melissa always played 'second fiddle' to Marjorie's first, settled for mediocre second-rate orchestras to Marjorie's national tours with renowned organizations, and collected Gumbys rather than Grammys.

So, the utterance of Melissa's name by Anton Rinaldi, that Marjorie heard 'clear-as-a-bell,' thanks to her enhanced hearing, was much more than just a mere dismissal. It was a slap in her professional face, a 'C' on her report card, chopsticks to her Chopin.

Internally mortified, but determined not to let it show, she rose from her piano's bench, methodically gathered her music, and strode out of the rehearsal hall, with her back straight and her head held high, like a queen exiting the cathedral after her coronation.

"If mediocre he wants, to compliment his mediocre composition, then they're a match made in H…," She mentally didn't want to finish the sentence she was thinking. She didn't want to stoop that low.

As Marjorie was exiting the building, lo and behold, who should be entering from the opposite direction but her nemesis, Melissa Crane. Having a difficult time assimilating the timeline for this encounter in relationship to her recent dismissal, Marjorie parried, as any good fencer would at the beginning of the match.

"Melissa."

"Marjorie."

"I see you're not letting any grass grow under your feet."

"The early bird does catch the worm."

"Tread carefully, the worm has fangs."

"I'm not afraid of any worm, with or without legs."

"Naturally, that's never stopped you before, has it?"

"I hope MY piano's in tune, this time."

"How would you know? The way you play, how could you possibly tell?"

This little 'tete-a-tete' (Fr.: head-to-head) continued well past the time that either woman could hear what the other was saying as they continued walking in opposite directions; even for Marjorie, who was wearing her new ear 'jewelry.' As Marjorie approached her car, parked in the neighboring garage, she had to admit to herself that if Melissa was here, now, that her recent dismissal was not spontaneous. This was planned. But why?

-- 1 week ago –

Time: 7 am

Location: Bedroom of Marjorie Cunningham

[ring, ring]

"Hello," Marjorie groaned into the phone, after the never ending 'looping' dream she was having was interrupted by the tumultuous ringing of her phone.

"Marjorie! Anton," he emphatically stated into the phone, as if she didn't already know who it was by the sound of his voice. A voice she immediately recognized, even without her hearing aids.

"What do you want?" she unceremoniously blurted into her end of the phone.

"Can we talk?" he asked.

"You can talk; I'll listen." she stated in conclusion, as her head reclaimed her pillow with the ear she wasn't using.

"Time has a way of making you look at things --differently," he began. "I've been looking at the Rhapsody, and it just doesn't sound right without you playing it," he admitted.

"Mellisa's all thumbs?" Marjorie hypothesized, as she held her mouth into the pillow to keep from giggling into the phone.

"She plays very well, don't get me wrong, but it just doesn't, -- it just doesn't, ---"

"Sing?" she inquired.

"Please come back. The Rhapsody needs you," he confessed, then pleaded into his end of the phone.

Marjorie was internally ecstatic over his admission, and overjoyed about the prospect of performing the Rhapsody, but she remained stoically silent for effect.

"Marjorie?" he inquired, after the long, unnerving silence continued.

"I'm still here; I'm thinking," she admitted, knowing she was in the driver's seat of this conversation.

"Would time and a half help make up your mind?" he asked.

"Time and a half, and -- thoughtful consideration by the conductor to my interpretive suggestions."

"Done," Anton said, relinquishing artistic control of his Rhapsody into the hands of the pianist, where they both knew it should have been from the beginning.

"See you tomorrow at 9," she stated, as she disconnected, then hugged her pillow to death.

Chapter 4

Doctor Eli Cassilly

Acoustic Engineer. PhD from Purdue University

In antiquity, when the Romans and the Greeks were constructing outdoor theaters for their comedies and dramas, as well as philosophical lectures, they utilized nature's natural formations to enhance not only sound's volume but the sound quality as well within their environment.

During medieval times, when theater goers preferred to be entertained indoors rather than outside, mechanical and civil engineers, using material readily available to them such as stone, wood and concrete, had to design spaces suitable to not only house the audience and participants, but to mechanically amplify sound as well.

Eli Cassilly, throughout his academic studies, was all too familiar with man's history of utilizing, creating, producing and manipulating sound to his advantage.

He's written many best-selling books on the subject. Just ask him; he'll tell you. But beyond being an expert on sounds' history, Doctor Cassilly has pioneered the use of modern acoustic technology to enhance the enjoyment of current aficionados by manipulating the very frequencies of sound itself. Many symphonic halls, the Meyerhoff included, have utilized Dr. Cassilly and his 'techniques,' to maximize the theater goer's experiences by constructing and tuning reflective baffles, which are hung from the ceiling(s) and mounted on the walls.

Generally speaking, the hall would be 'tuned' and adjusted for maximum effect when the full orchestra was on stage, thus conveying and enhancing <u>their</u> sound throughout the building. Once this was accomplished, the baffles were locked in place, Dr. Cassilly's job was complete, and he could venture forth to perform his 'miracle' at another prestigious symphony hall, in another lucrative city. With other forms and styles of music however, i.e., chamber orchestras, stringed quartets and solo recitals for example, the main hall would not be 'tuned' for their particular genre. They were therefore relegated to side venues more suitably 'tuned' for their needs. The increased popularity of those very same entities, however, put the symphony's Board of Trustees in an uncomfortable conundrum. To maximize monetary intake from those performances, they needed to utilize the main hall, which was unfortunately not 'tuned' for them, specifically. In order to accomplish the goal of 'making more money,' the Board of Trustees at the Meyerhoff decided that the hall needed to be 'tuned' for every performance. Naturally, this meant logistically scheduling, then combining the hall's performances into specific genres. After all, they did have a limited budget. Then, subsequently, re-hire Dr. Cassilly to perform his magic.

This was naturally good news for Dr. Cassilly, i.e., more work, greater income. On the surface, that is. It also meant longer working hours for him, and the necessity to have to deal with and endure the dispositions of more individual musicians, over and above that of the orchestra's conductor.

-- 5 years ago –

Time: 8 am
Location: Meyerhoff Symphony Hall
Purpose: Tuning the hall for a piano recital
Performer: Marjorie Cunningham (aidless)

"A little to the right, -- that's it, now down 1.25 inches," advised Dr. Cassilly of his technicians, who were supported by forklifts at ceiling level, while he remained at the acoustic resonance attenuation console in the control room.

Those types of commands, shouted back and forth between the acoustic engineer and his staff all day, could be heard echoing throughout the hall, even though they were using handheld and head mounted electronic communication gear. Constant prattle, as far as Marjorie was concerned, while she endured having to play the unending music for her upcoming performance from the stage below where they were working, on the recently tuned piano, in order for Dr. Cassilly to 'tune' the hall.

After endless minutes of this, which seemed like hours to her, Marjorie called over to her understudy, who was observing the proceedings from the wings, to come and take her place at the keyboard. This finally allowed Marjorie not only to rest her hands, but to meander around the hall and see for herself what all the technical fuss was all about.

Perambulating into all the nooks and crannies that made up the Meyerhoff Symphony Hall, she noticed, and rather quickly, that the piano's resident tones waxed and waned in volume and quality depending on where she stood. She was also quite aware that Dr. Cassilly, and his minions, had departed from her side of the concert hall and were concentrating their talents elsewhere. As the performer, she thought she should bring this discrepancy of the hall's acoustic variation to the attention of the audio engineer.

"You don't say," was Dr. Cassilly's answer to Marjorie's observations.

"I do say," claimed Marjorie in retort after receiving Cassilly's short and dismissive answer.

"And who are you again to be criticizing the acoustic engineer?" he snidely asked.

"I'm the pianist for this concert," she stated.

"Then shouldn't you be playing the piano, where you belong, and not up here bothering me," he condescendingly suggested.

She quickly realized that any further discussions on the subject would be futile and strode out of the sound booth. At first, she thought about taking his advice, then changed her mind. Bypassing the stage entrance, she walked directly into the president-of-the-board's office. To her surprise, she found the president in conversation with the music director, Anton Rinaldi.

"Oh, good," she exclaimed. "You've just saved me the time to come and look for you." The two men just stared at each other, not knowing what she was talking about.

She went on to explain to them both what she heard, or didn't hear, and the reaction of Dr. Cassilly when she brought this, the hall's acoustic problems, to his attention. She then very strongly suggested that they follow her to see/hear for themselves. Having very little choice in the matter, representing the Meyerhoff's fiscal as well as reputational aspects were concerned, they followed her into the concert hall. There, she showed them the various sections of the hall that were, in her opinion, void of, or diminished in, auditory volume and quality. They, to their bewilderment, and her astonishment, had to agree. Knowing they were paying an inordinate amount of money to Dr. Cassilly for his, 'expertise' in this arena, they made a point of immediately bringing this 'deficit' to his attention. Needless to say, Dr. Cassilly was not at all pleased with what they had to vocalize concerning his expertise, nor about Marjorie Cunningham, personally.

From that day on, which became fewer here or elsewhere, whenever the Meyerhoff utilized Dr. Cassilly and his tuning 'techniques,' extra care and attention was paid by the powers-that-be to the outcomes, especially when Marjorie Cunningham, Dr. Cassilly's less than favorite pianist, was on the bill.

-- One week ago –

Time: 11 am

Location: Meyerhoff Symphony Hall
Purpose: Tuning the hall for a piano/orchestral recital
Performer: Marjorie Cunningham (enhanced)

As the orchestra, with Marjorie Cunningham at the piano, rehearsed from the mainstage Anton's Rhapsody in C, Marjorie couldn't help but gaze into the atrium to observe Dr. Cassily and his crew adjusting and readjusting the multitude of giant domed, 10-foot spherical discs hanging from the ceiling throughout the building.

As per her usual behavior, where Dr. Cassilly was concerned, she beckoned her understudy to take her place at the keyboard so that she might peruse the hall. And she was not alone. Dozens of technicians, with handheld Prosonic Sound Decimal Meters, were combing the nooks and crannies as well.

From Cassilly's vantage point in the 'rafters,' if looks could have killed, Marjorie Cunningham would be dead.

Chapter 5

Jonah Pyke

Registered Piano Technician (RPT); Member of Piano Technicians Guild (PTG); MS from University of Houston

-- 5 years ago --

Time: 8 am
Location: Meyerhoff Symphony Hall
Purpose: Tuning the Steinway for a piano recital
Performer: Marjorie Cunningham

She usually didn't get up this early on a Saturday, nor attend the tuning of her piano prior to a concert in person, but in this case, she wanted to be at the Symphony Hall before the piano tuner arrived. She usually didn't stick her nose in the mechanical care and maintenance of her instrument either, but in this case, she was making an exception. Through the powers that be, she had come to learn that Jonah Pyke, the registered piano technician, was going to be tuning her instrument today prior to her concert this evening. She had the unfortunate pleasure of having to deal with this particular piano tuner in the past, at another venue, which consequently resulted not only in a very nervous and stilted performance on her part, and what could only be described as a tolerable experience for the audience, but the necessity to report him to the technicians guild where he received a stern reprimand and censure.

Granted, it was an outdoor concert, and that for any stringed instrument requires extra precautions, but the instrument should have been checked just prior to the performance, which didn't happen, because the tech, Jonah Pyke, had left the venue. Normally, once the tech checks and tunes the piano, earlier in the day, he/she would check it again just prior to the concert, i.e., within minutes. In this case, from the time he tuned it, early in the morning, to the time it needed to be played, later that evening, it not only untuned itself but acquired not one but two 'sticky keys.' Once discovered by the pianist, in this case, Marjorie Cunningham, at the very onset of the performance, which, as she attested to at his hearing, "only took her seconds," the problems could have judiciously and professionally been fixed. With him not in attendance whatsoever, the concert had to be played ---'As is.'

It was also suggested that the piano might not have been 'tuned' or maintained correctly from the onset. Mr. Pyke's unprofessional history also came to light at the hearing supporting this contention.

Regardless, the show 'needed-to-go-on,' and it did so very awkwardly and painfully. Marjorie, becoming all too aware of the piano's shortcomings immediately, did her professional best to minimize the problems. Using dynamics and phrasing, not to mention pausing intentionally, to minimize the stuck keys, only worked so well. The out-of-tune strings, however, were a completely different problem. She did her utmost to maintain poise and decorum, along with maintaining a 'poker face' throughout the entire concert, to assuage any misgivings of atonality the audience thought they might be hearing. But alas, minuscule constant dissonances 'does-not-a-good-concert-make.' And when she found out that the Hall had hired Jonah Pyke as tech for <u>this</u> concert, she made damn sure she would be here, in person, to supervise her instruments care. She didn't want to have to go through a night of embarrassment like she was subjected to in the past.

As she was reliving a not so very cherished moment from that past, while perched on the lip of the main stage, the man of her daydream wandered into the hall. Looking like he had just climbed out of bed, bedraggled in appearance and ambulating askew down the aisle, through half lidded eye slots, he just about recognized the figure seated on the stage when he pronounced:

"Aw, it's you," he intoned, sarcastically, as he deposited his tool laden valise upon the stage itself. "What are you doing here? As if I didn't already know," he bemoaned.

"And a good morning to you, too," she retorted, handing him a steaming hot Styrofoam cup of coffee.

"What's this, a peace offering?" he chided.

"Hardly," she countered. "I just wanted to make sure that you were wide awake this morning before you applied your trade to my instrument, in earnest," she projected.

"That's very thoughtful of you," he surmised. But he had an underlying suspicion that she was dead-serious.

"Not at all. I always make it my business to look after the people who look after me."

Now he knew she was playing with him. "Look! I'm sorry about what happened to your piano at that . . ."

"Let's not revisit and rehash the past. What's done is done. Let's just make sure it doesn't happen again. Like tonight, let's say." As she finished her monologue, she hoisted her own cup of coffee up a few inches in front of her face.

Taking that gesture and statement as a sign of peace, he did likewise.

"Shall we get started?" she suggested.

Setting down his cup on the lip of the stage, which in and of itself was a corporate 'no-no,' he hoisted his tuning wrench out of his bag and saluted her properly with it.

Two hours later, after completing several runs, through various sections of the score, Marjorie ceased playing after being totally convinced that her piano was perfect. Or, as perfect as a human being could make it. After gleefully sliding off the piano's bench, she replaced her derriere in the very spot on stage she had occupied earlier in the day.

"Staying for the concert?" she inquired with a smirk on her face.

"Are you kidding?" replied Jonah, who was residing in seat one of the first row watching her rehearse.

"Wouldn't miss it for the world."

--Present day –

Time: 8 am

Location: Meyerhoff Symphony Hall
Purpose: Tuning the Steinway for a piano recital
Performer: Marjorie Cunningham (enhanced)

After bidding an enthusiastic good morning to the security guard at the front door, Marjorie found herself skipping into the main hall of the Joseph Meyerhoff Symphony complex. Bounding toward the stage, she came up short when she realized she wasn't alone. There on the stage, elbows deep inside the harp strings of the full-sized Steinway, with his butt projecting toward her, his only audience, like a performers' spotlight, was Jonah Pyke. Upon hearing the pitter patter of little feet, Jonah emerged from the piano's depths to address his only fan. As the piano's two caretakers advanced on each other, Jonah from the stage, Marjorie up the aisle, Jonah reached the upstage lip of the apron first. This allowed him to bend over, and after reaching into a bag that was residing there, produced a steaming 'lidded' mug of coffee.

"I thought you might be needing this," he proclaimed, with a smirk on his face.

"I always knew you were preceptive. S'about time you let it show," she teased, accepting the proffered mug.

"You're late. I've already started," he jibed.

"I can see this," she countered, climbing up onto the stage with his help.

Two hours later, after completing several passes through various sections of the score, as per usual, Marjorie ceased playing, after being totally convinced that her piano was -- perfect.

Moderately enthusiastic hand clapping could be heard coming from the only patron seated in the first row. Jonah stood, while still clapping, in order to help Marjorie jump down from the almost four-foot-high stage.

"You _are_ coming tonight?" asked a hopeful pianist.

In answer to her question, Jonah pulled out a non-refundable, pristine admission ticket from his breast pocket which read:

Section A; Row 1; Seat 1

Jonah, with a big smile on his face, plopped down into the very seat he had just vacated, and while waving the ticket at her, smiled.

How could she help but smile in return.

Music

Chapter 6

Music Therapy 101

Date: One year ago

Time: 8 pm

Location: University of Maryland Medical Schools' Department of Social Services lecture Hall, Baltimore, MD

Purpose: Lecture on Entrainment

"I've always included music into my practice," claimed the Speech-Language Pathologist (SLP) to the Social Worker (SW) as they chatted while waiting for the official lecture to start. "It's played a large part in enhancing focus in my developmentally challenged individuals," claimed the SLP. "Especially with my clientele on the spectrum."

"Same here. With all the domestic violent cases I've worked with over the years, I've always found that soft Baroque music playing in the background of my office, especially Vivaldi, rendered my clients more amenable to negotiation and less prone to arguing," admitted the SW. "Truth be told, I think J.S. Bach saved my life once when a wife was just about to physically strike her husband, right there in my office, when a passage from 'Air on a G string,' no pun intended, wove its way through my office and distracted her. For a minute there,

I thought I was going to have to call the police. Bach's my hero."

"I've had similar experiences myself with my more, shall I say, aggressive ADHD (Attention Deficit/Hyperactivity Disorder) individuals. They feel anger and frustration more intensely and therefore act out more rapidly in situations than others might," claimed the SLP. "And I've been using music as a way to channel calmness into those individuals using rhythm, tempo and even song to enhance focus and clarity; even promote calmness."

While they were talking, a woman who had just entered made her way down the aisle and took up the empty seat next to the SLP.

"And, speaking of music, the angel without her harp has now joined the fray. This is the pianist I've told you about who is helping me in my practice. Without her, I don't think I would have had as many positive outcomes over the last few years as I have."

The SP introduced the pianist to the SW.

"I've heard a lot of good things about you," claimed the SW. "Your reputation precedes you."

"You're just saying that because it's true," joked the pianist, half-heartedly.

"I thought as a professional pianist, you wouldn't have the time to invest in music therapy sessions," asked the SW.

"One would think. But it's not a matter of time, it's a matter of money," admitted the pianist.

Before the SW could 'grill' the pianist any more concerning the current national pay grade average for pianists, the MC for the evening began to address the gathered audience. This brought all non-essential chit-chat to a halt. The MC then introduced the speaker for the evening, and the lecture officially began.

Billed as an expert in her field and the author of numerous books on the subject, the lecturer proceeded to explain to those gathered the main topic of her presentation: Entrainment.

She went on to explain that entrainment is the process by which two independent rhythmic or fluid systems synchronize or interact. She then gave numerous examples where entrainment could be found, from biology, physics, in social interactions and astrology.

Specific examples included:

1)   Biology, as pertains to the Circadian rhythm. Where aligning sleep-wake cycles could be achieved by aligning light-dark cycles.

2)   Neuro-physiologically, where the use of rhythmic stimuli like binaural beats or flickering lights could guide brain activity toward a specific frequency, thus resulting in greater relaxation and focus.

3)   Psychosocial behavior, in which individuals unconsciously can synchronize their movements or speech patterns during social interactions.

4)   Mechanically. A classic example of this would be when two pendulum clocks, mounted on the same wall, eventually swing in sync.

5)   Meteorologically, where a hyperactive, turbulent storm captures a non-turbulent one and creates a third, altogether.

The lecture and the lecturer were riveting. The subject matter was fascinating and touched base on a variety of medical and scientific subjects which resonated with as many varied medical and scientific personnel in the audience. Everyone came away from the lecture with ideas of how to utilize entrainment in their chosen fields.

The lecturer, after her presentation, received a well-deserved standing ovation, and could hardly get off the stage with all the attention she was receiving from the audience.

Eventually, when she finally made her way over to where the SLP and SW were lauding her praises, the SW, in keeping with societal decorum, introduced everyone in their company:

"Melissa Crane, professional pianist, may I formally introduce you to our expert guest speaker and renowned audiologist, Dr. Felice Hoeman."

Chapter 7

The Rhapsody in C

Date: Present day

Time: 8 pm

Location: Joseph Meyerhoff Symphony Hall, Baltimore MD

Despite the ongoing contentious rehearsals that took place between herself and the conductor/composer, once she was back at her keyboard, the end-product proved worth the confrontations. Marjorie's suggestions regarding the interpretation of the Rhapsody, more often-than-not, were implemented by Anton, which garnered positive results. All told, the Rhapsody was magnificent.

Everyone, especially Anton, was more than anxious for the world to hear what they were about to premiere.

Months prior to tonight, just after her auditory fittings, Marjorie took Claire's advice and began letting her hair grow out. And she was glad that she did. Now, with it well past shoulder length, no one would ever guess that she was wearing bilateral hearing aids. As foretold by both the audiologist, as well as Claire, the aids not only worked as promised, but brought back to Marjorie the appreciation of all that was musical, from the minuscule chirp of a cricket to the blast of a ship's horn, and every previously indistinct nuance in between. She did, however, regret being able to hear the soft gossip shared between members of the orchestra, when they thought that no one could hear them; but the tradeoff was worth it.

Word had spread, in the musical and secular communities alike, concerning the recent chasms that had been bridged between Anton Rinaldi and Marjorie Cunningham, and it showed. The lobby of the Meyerhoff was packed with theater goers tighter than sardines in a can. Reporters lined-the-avenues leading into the complex, interviewing anyone that could be quoted as having had a hand in tonight's gala. Television crews were capturing scenes of party goers from the average person on the street to the mayor of the city. The Meyerhoff's façade had been adorned with colored lights and banners depicting the likenesses of both Anton Rinaldi and Marjorie Cunningham, as well as proclaiming the world premiere of a new piece of music.

In attendance for tonight's performance, besides the usual 'who's-who' from the governor and members of the state and city's political hierarchy to the Archbishop of Baltimore, was Jake Rivers, Private Detective, and his wife Nina. Accompanying them, en masse, and celebrating their first completed year of connubial bliss, following their Argentinian nuptials, was his partner Patrick Murphy and his wife Marguerite, Jake and Nina's daughter Tanya, and her husband David Middlestat, and Colonel Robert Lamm and his wife Catherine (Katie). Keeping an eye on the entire entourage, to prevent them from getting into trouble, as he would claim if asked, was Lieutenant Tony McCall and his wife Bridget. As the Rivers clan jostled into position within their box seats on the first tier, in preparation for the performance, orchestra members were jostling into position upon the stage. In their respective dressing rooms, Anton Rinaldi was opening the last of his congratulatory cards and telegrams, and Marjorie Cunningham was performing the last of her finger warm-up exercises. Earlier that day, she had already enlisted and undertook to practice the 80/20 rule in music, also known as the Pareto Principle, which states that 80% of results come from 20% of efforts. Or, in this case, 80% of mistakes often stem from 20% of the music's difficult passages. As such, she always identified and drilled those sections of the music to minimize her time rehearsing in order to maximize proficient outcomes. Satisfied that she knew the piece as well as it could be performed, she took one last look in the mirror, to make sure that her appearance was as good as it could be, then left the dressing room and headed into the wings. There, she was met by Anton, who, after extending to her his hand, accompanied by a large smile, remarked,

"Break a leg."

"It's a magnificent piece of music, you should be proud," she said in a congratulatory manner while returning the handshake. Formal salutations having been dispensed with, the two of them had only to wait for the 'go ahead,' then proceed to their respective performers positions on stage to make it so.

Meanwhile, in the front upper box seating area, the assembled family members were thanking Jake and Tony for tonight's anniversary gift tickets they had bestowed upon them earlier, to celebrate the one-year wedding anniversaries of Murph and Marguerite, David and Tanya, and Michael and Katie. The men shook hands; the women kissed the women; the women kissed the men. Generally speaking, Jake could just imagine the scuttlebutt that must have been circulating around the theater at that moment, i.e., having the city's 'who's-who' wondering, if not openly being jealous of, all the PDAs (Public Display of Affection) they witnessed taking place in Box 1A.

As the lights dimmed, the audience quieted. The concert 'A' was sounded, and the musicians matched their respective instrument's frequency with the resounding 440 Hz. After which, there was silence.

Backstage, Marjorie took a deep breath and proceeded to enter the stage from the wings. Before she could do so, a gentle but firm hand on her elbow stopped her. She turned to see Anton shaking his head in the negative. He intentionally and insistently guided her behind him and beckoned her to wait. He then proceeded to precede her onto the stage, letting her take the prestigious final entrance befitting a soloist of her caliber over the Rhapsody's composer.

The audience, taking their cue from his entrance, gave him, and all that his station deserved, their acknowledgement and thanks.

Marjorie, dumbfounded by the sincere gesture, stood immobile in the wings. Immobile, until a stagehand tapped her on the arm, and, as silently as a mime, indicated to her that the concert couldn't begin if she didn't ambulate to the piano. Thanking him with a smile and a silent nod, she ventured forth.

No sooner did the bottom of her gown enter the lights of the stage did the audience respond accordingly. Foot stomping, bow tapping, and whistling, intermingled with the thunderous applause emanating from the SRO (standing room only) crowd. Not many people alive can claim the breathtaking moment Marjorie experienced that evening as she walked over to shake the conductor's hand, amidst a reception such as this, not even Marjorie herself.

Humbled beyond words, she gathered her wits and composed her nerves; graciously curtsied her thanks to the audience, winked at Jonah Pyke, who was seated in the first row, then took her place at the piano.

The moment of truth was at hand. Akin to anticipating the sound of the starter's pistol at any sporting event, was the deafening silence heard within seconds just after the conductor's baton was raised.

Over the next forty-five minutes, the Rhapsody ebbed and flowed through uplifting melodious patterns, only to be taken apart and contradicted by variations, then reunited again and cherished. Multiple themes and counter points had the audience mesmerized, and wondering where all the variations were taking them, only to be pleasantly surprised at the masterfully arranged segues leading to the conclusion. And the conclusion was anticipated by one and all.

Sensing they were being led toward the climax, the emotional tension of everyone throughout the hall was palpable. Marjorie's hands and fingers were difficult to focus on, by those within viewing distance, because of the shear speed at which they were traveling. True to its namesake, the growing predominance of the pitch 'C' was being toyed with, then harmonically moved away from, only to coalesce again on the root of the Rhapsody.

Urgent and faster was the tempo; louder and more robust was its nature. Cascades and crescendos followed the multiple arpeggios across the keyboard. Margorie was bounding across her bench in the vain attempt to keep up with her hands. The hands that were beginning to sweat. The sweat that not only could she feel everywhere, but that was also noticeable to the audience as well.

Anton looked askance at Marjorie just then, because her playing was becoming uncharacteristically erratic and faster than his stick. Her face was reddening, and her breathing was quickening and could be physically heard by those around her. Especially focused on what was transpiring on stage, from her vantage point in the theater was Katie. As a medically trained, combat EMT, she recognized an unnatural 'state-of-being' when presented with the symptoms. She immediately looked askew at her mentor and fellow combat EMT, Lieutenant Tony McCall, who upon recognizing the same symptoms, was mirroring that same concerned look of comprehension.

As Marjorie's playing became more erratic, the tell-tale signs of pain could be seen etched across her face, as her hands seemed to move on their own, regardless of the tempo set by conductor and orchestra alike.

"Something's wrong," stated Katie as she slowly rose from her chair in the balcony and began to make her way out into the hallway. Tony was right on her heals, and he was quickly followed by Bridget, the RN.

Before either one of them could make their way down to the stage, Marjorie stood from where she was playing, grabbed the side of her head with respective hands, and with a scream that rent the auditorium's sonic veil asunder, collapsed face first onto the stage.

Jonah Pyke, being the closest bystander, was the first to reach her side after leaping up on the stage. Not being medically trained, he was at a loss to know what to do for her, especially when observing the torrent of blood that was cascading out of both eyes, nostrils, mouth and ears simultaneously.

By then, Katie, Tony, and Bridget had reached the apron of the stage and were thundering across its downstage lip flashing credentials and calling for everyone to **"Backup!"** Coming up short themselves, after recognizing the possible signs and symptoms of hemorrhagic fever, i.e., Eboli, they instructed everyone within earshot to back away from Marjorie as quickly as possible. Bridget was on her cellphone calling 911 as Katie and Tony, who had donned latex gloves (which they always carried on their person) carefully examined Marjorie.

It was blatantly obvious to them that she was dead: no pulse, no respiration, non-responsive pupils. All they could do now was keep the masses calm and wait for the ambulance.

Chapter 8

D.S. al Coda

By the time Jake and Murph had arrived on the scene, Tony and Katie had managed to quadrant off a good 8-foot circular perimeter around the fallen pianist that no one was allowed to enter. The police had arrived by then and had temporarily sealed the building. Jonah Pyke, looking lost and distraught, retook his seat down front. The musicians, with instruments in hand, were slowly and apprehensively making their way off the mainstage and into the wings, with periodic, mournful, over-the-shoulder glances toward where Marjorie lie, uncharacteristically still on the floor. Anton Rinaldi was consoling those orchestra members that appeared more stricken than most and needed some guidance and support at this moment. His stoic demeanor, in the face of tragedy, lent a well needed anchor for those in distress that were floundering.

A young woman, outwardly grieving, had made her way to the apron and was allowing the stage itself to keep her erect.

"Claire!" Bridget exclaimed from the stage, after recognizing her coworker.

"Bridget?" came the woman's reply, as the two made their way into each other's arms.

"What are you doing here?" asked a concerned Bridget.

"It's my aunt," Claire bemoaned into Bridget's shoulder, after a quick glance at the stage.

"Your aunt?" Bridget queried, not mentally connecting the surname of 'Cunningham with Adams,' until now.

"Oh Claire, I'm so sorry," Bridget empathically intoned, as she gave her colleague a tighter hug.

By this time, Tony and Katie had relinquished their guardianship of Marjorie over to the police, and had joined Jake and Murph at Bridget's side. As Claire was drying her eyes after being released from Bridget's embrace, Bridget took the opportunity to introduce Claire to her family.

"Claire, this is Tony, my husband, and Katie Lamm. They're both ex-military and combat EMT's. And this is Jake Rivers and Patrick Murphy, private investigators. Claire Adams, RN, Marjorie Cunningham's niece."

"Miss Adams, I'm so sorry for your loss," sincerely admitted Tony, whose facial expression and body language was emulated by the entire, recently introduced entourage.

"Miss Adams. Has your aunt been out of the country recently?" asked a concerned Katie.
"No," stated Claire emphatically. "She's been too busy performing concerts and preparing for this one."

The medical professionals in attendance absorbed and acknowledged the implied information. This same 'fact' was not missed by Jake or Murph collectively either.

"I don't understand any of this," sobbed Claire. "Other than having slightly elevated blood pressure and a moderate hearing loss, she was in perfect health. I oversaw her physical examination at the hospital a little over six months ago. I just don't understand any of this," she repeated. "How was this possible?" she just managed to say again before collapsing back into Bridget's arms.

"That's what the coroner's going to tell us, Miss Adams," stated Murph, as he watched the paramedics who had finally arrived, hermetically sealed in hazmat suits, lift Marjorie's inert body onto the gurney and cover it with a white sheet.

"So, what you're saying, if I understand you correctly, is that the likelihood of your aunt having Eboli or other possible sources of hemorrhagic fever is remote to none?" asked Jake of Claire.

"Absolutely," claimed Claire, as she came off Bridget's shoulder for air.

Murph looked over at Jake just then and declared:

"I'll inform the coroner as soon as I get a chance."

"Excuse me," said Jonah Pyke, interjecting himself into the conversation. "My name's Jonah Pyke, I'm Marjorie Cunningham's piano technician, and I couldn't help but overhear your conversation. I can substantiate Miss Adams' statements. I've been working with Marjorie for years, and specifically over this last week preparing for this concert, and I've never seen her even catch a cold much less be ill."

After making his statement, he turned his attention to Claire. "Miss Adams, I can't tell you how much your aunt meant to me. I'm, -- I'm, --" and he couldn't finish articulating his feelings, being obviously upset. Claire released Bridget to take hold of Jonah's hands, and the two just stood there in silent, mutual commiseration.

Michael Lamm, secondary to the thinning crowd, had finally made his way to the stage and came up to stand beside his wife.

"Katie?" he asked, sensing something, amiss, and received no reply.

"Katie?" asked Murph of his niece, who was projecting a look that he hadn't seen her wear in a long time.

After sheepishly looking around at all the family members who were present, Katie, after remembering back to when she was twelve years old at the Lyric theater, commented,

"Is it just me, or do these things seem to happen only when I'm around?"

The Sign

Chapter 9

Pam Richardson, Sgt. Detective in the homicide division of Baltimore's downtown police, strolled across the street early this morning with a caramel macchiato in hand, headed for the central police station. Over the years she'd been stationed there, unlike others that called the station home, she never did acquire the taste for the precinct's coffee. God knows she tried to ingest the swill they'd all come to love, but to her, it was more akin to a combination of ashtray liquid, toilet water and shoe polish. She'd rather take the gibing from the local boys-in-blue, than swallow a proffered mug of precinct 'Joe.'

After hanging up her coat, she walked around the all-to-familiar 'man-mountain' seated at the desk right across from hers and took up her usual place behind her desk.

"Hey Murph," she intoned in greeting, as naturally, and as nonchalantly as she would take in an inspiration of air. It took her quite a while to realize what she had said, and to whom she said it, before she reared back into her chair, almost knocking her precious golden liquid all over her morning reports.

"MURPH!" she cried. What the . . ., what in the hell are you doing here?" she exclaimed all buggy-eyed, just before she threw herself across both desks to land in his lap and crush him in a gigantic bear hug.

"You know, all you're doing is giving them more ammunition for gossip," he claimed as he tried, half-heartedly, to detach her from his being. After only a few seconds of beratement, he relented and hugged her right back.

"What's up?" she asked, as she dismounted the 'man-mountain,' and walked her way back over to her chair, in the vain attempt to pretend her recent outburst of emotion didn't happen and wasn't noticed by everyone. She failed, miserably. The same could be said for Murph. No one within viewing distance cared, because everyone understood.

"I was headed over to the coroner's office and thought I'd stop by to say, 'hi,'" he claimed.

"Well, 'hey' right back at 'cha," she declared.

"Does this have to do with that death the other night at the Meyerhoff?" she inquired.

"One and the same," he admitted. "How did you know?" he asked.

"Friends of mine where there at the concert that night and saw you and Jake chatting front-and-center with some notables right after, well, --- right after."

"Yeah, we gave the ME some information concerning the deceased, and he called me yesterday and asked if I'd stop by. You know me, ear to the pavement . . .,"

"Nose to the grindstone," she concluded.

"Have you heard anything?" he asked.

"No official word of inquiry has hit the fan yet. Maybe after your little tat-to-tat with the coroner you could, -- you know."

"Yeah, yeah, you'll be the first to know," claimed Murph in response, as he rose from his chair and stretched. "I may have missed you guys, but my back sure as heck hasn't missed that chair," he claimed, as he waved 'bye' over his shoulder and headed down the steps.

"Tell everyone I said, 'hi,' she insisted,

"Will do," he declared as a final salutation, before being lost from view.

The coroner, seeing a familiar face stroll into his examination room, waved Murph back to his private office.

"Murph, how the hell are you?" inquired the ME while extending his hand in welcome.

"You know me Doc," Murph admitted, taking the proffered hand in his.

"Yeah, I do. Have a seat," he requested, indicating one of the chairs nearby.

"I take it you have some news?" asked Murph.

"You could say that, and then yet again," and he let the sentence hang.

This 'non-admission' peeked Murph's interest more than 'in-hand' facts.

"The info you passed on to me the other night turned out to be factual. The woman didn't have Eboli or any other form of hemorrhagic disease. In fact, she was relatively healthy," admitted the ME. "Her organs were intact and matched, if not superseded her chronological age."

"Then, --- what?" Murph inquired.

"Murph, you're rushing me, and you know how I hate to be rushed," the ME jovially remarked.

Murph took the hint, and kept his mouth shut.

"Murph," the ME began, as he reclined back into his chair, "in all the years as a medical examiner, I've never seen anything like this. Well, that's not exactly true, but I'll get to that in a minute."

"The woman died of massive, and by massive, I mean extensive, universal rupture of every arteriole in her brain, eyes and ears."

"But isn't that what hemorrhagic disease does?" Murph asked.

"No," exclaimed the ME. "With Eboli and its related diseases, the organs are literally eaten, liquify, then escape through any orifice it can find. In this case," and he paused to make sure that Murph understood, "the vessels exploded, simultaneously."

Murph just sat there not knowing what to ask.

"If it was a weakness in the walls of the vessels, like an aneurysm, a sudden increase in blood pressure, which, by the way did occur, could rupture that particular structure. In this case, every small artery in her brain, eyes and ears ruptured, simultaneously. If it was a matter of a systemic reaction to a drug, let's say, that spiked her blood pressure, the resultant increase in arterial pressure would find weak spots in her anatomy and create failure therein. Even if it were so, it would only last for a brief span of time and you would have seen a cavalcading destruction throughout the body in various locations. This was not like that. This was localized and targeted."

Murph sat there for a few seconds, before he rationalized, "When you say, "targeted," do you mean, "criminally?"

"I'm not at liberty to make that statement, yet. All I can say now, is that her death was not 'natural.'

Murph sat back in his chair just then and steepled his fingers under his lips.

"I've only seen this type, this 'pattern' of destruction once before, when I was in the army, and they brought to me victims of gamma radiation from a nuclear blast. There, topographic dermal cells were instantaneously exposed to intense energy from the splitting of atoms, then subsequently destroyed. This is quite similar, but very specific, and just as deadly."

"Shit," Murph exclaimed.

"That's putting it mildly," concluded the ME.

"Is that why you haven't enlisted the cops?" asked Murph. "You can't finalize the death certificate?"

"Exactly," remarked the doctor. "There are some other avenues I what to pursue, and tests I need to run, but until then, I have to treat this as a natural death."

"<u>You</u> might, but <u>I</u> don't have to," exclaimed Murph, as he stood from his chair.

"I hoped you'd say that," concluded the ME, as he reached out and shook the hand Murph had offered.

"I'll be in touch, Doc,"

"Same here, Murph. Give Jake my best."

"Will do, Doc. Will do."

Chapter 10

Accelerando

"Shit!" uttered Jake.

"That's what I said," claimed Murph, after he explained to Jake what the coroner had explained to him.

"Marguerite!" Jake called. Before either man could move a muscle, the door to Jake's office opened and Marguerite, Jake's secretary, Murph's wife, with a tray ladened with three glasses and a decanter of the 'good stuff,' walked in.

After three glasses were wordlessly poured, then toasted with and slowly drained, Murph turned to Jake and said:

"Now you know why I keep her around."

This comment was quickly followed by Marguerite pulling Murph's ear, then subsequently planting a kiss to the top of his forehead. As she made her way out of the room, to allow the men to continue their discussions, she stopped off to give Babe, who was singing a lovely snake tune from her aquarium, a caress. She left the decanter.

Not too long thereafter, Marguerite interrupted their deliberations by announcing over the intercom:

"Jake, Bridget is here with Miss Adams."

Jake and Murph exchanged looks which begged the question, *"Speak of the devil, how did they know we were talking about them?"*

"Send them in," Jake requested of Marguerite, in order to solve the unspoken question that was 'hanging-in-the-air.'

Bridget and Claire, still dressed in their hospital scrubs, were escorted into the room by Marguerite, where they were offered chairs by 'Jake Rivers & Associate.'

"And pray tell, what brings two lovely 'nurses' to our humble establishment?" Jake began, as both Murph and Jake kissed Bridget on the cheek and shook Claire's hand before the women took their seats. "Nice to see you again, Miss Adams," Jake said concluding his salutation.

"Claire and I just finished a shift at the hospital together and I asked her over to the house for dinner. On the way, we began to talk about her aunt and the unusual circumstances of her death. Claire said she wanted to speak to you about that, and I told her that we would be passing this way on our travels to my house and, well, here we are," admitted Bridget.

Jake and Murph then turned their attention to Claire, indicating to her that they were 'all-ears,' and that the floor was 'all-hers.'

"I can't get out of my mind how untimely, and as far as I'm concerned, unnaturally my aunt died," she began. "I haven't heard anything from the police, as yet, and to be honest, I wonder if I ever will. I've never been involved with anything like this before, but I can't shake the feeling that something is amiss; that I, personally, need to be doing something. Maybe it's just the 'not knowing' that has me worried. Does that make any sense?" she asked.

"It makes perfect sense," admitted Jake, with a nod of approval from Murph.

"As a matter of fact, we were just talking about your aunt before you came in," claimed Murph.

Now it was the women's turn to look baffled.

Jake nodded his head, giving Murph the 'go ahead' to speak.

"I spoke with the coroner just recently, who conveyed to me his concern that your aunt didn't die of natural causes."

Claire exchanged a quick glance at Bridget before putting both hands up to her mouth and exclaiming:

"I knew it!"

"Now let's not jump to any conclusions. The coroner's just speculating at this time, and there needs to be more investigations into the matter," stated Jake.

"But the police aren't involved yet, are they?" asked Bridget.

"No. Because the cause of death cannot be officially determined, yet. As such, the police remain on 'standby,'" admitted Murph.

"But <u>you</u> could investigate, couldn't you, Mr. Rivers?" asked a tearful Claire, wiping her eyes dry with a tissue.

Jake and Murph exchanged thoughtful and hopeful expressions, just before Jake answered:

"We could, Miss Adams; once someone asks us."

Claire stood just then and extended her hand across the desk which separated her from Jake, declaring:

"Then consider yourself asked, Mr. Rivers."

Chapter 11

Crescendo

Closing her coat against the chill of the morning air, Melissa Crane scampered up the steps of the Meyerhoff already late for this morning's rehearsal. Despite the recent demise of their concert soloist, Marjorie Cunningham, the Meyerhoff had the Rhapsody of Anton Rinaldi scheduled for six more performances on its main stage this week, and six more performances the following week at the Music Center at Strathmore, located in North Bethesda. They also had multimillion dollar investments in the Rapsody's national tour, scheduled thereafter, which was now in serious jeopardy of defaulting under contract, due to the lack of a pianist.

The Board of Trustees communicated their concerns to its music director, who just happened to be the Rapsody's composer, who in turn requested that Melissa Crane take Marjorie's place. She, more than happily acquiesced, and was currently making her way into the hall for the unscheduled, now scheduled rehearsal prior to tonight's uncancelled performance.

Before she could enter the building's interior however, a voice, accompanied by a tall figure, interrupted her line of travel.

"Miss Crane, do you mind if I have a word with you?"

"Well, I'm already late for rehearsal and I don't know . . ,"

"I won't take up much of your time, I would just like to ask you a few questions about your taking over for Marjorie Cunningham." asked the stranger.

Taken slightly aback by this statement, because not many people, inside or outside the business, to date, knew of her acceding to the role vacated by Marjorie, she paused to ask:

"And you are?"

"Jake Rivers, Private Investigator," he claimed, as he handed to her his business card.

She hesitated to touch the card, which did not go unnoticed.

"And why would a private investigator be interested in the role a pianist was taking in the course of her musical career?" she asked in turn.

"Because according to your professors and colleagues in school and in the field alike, you and Marjorie have had a very, let's just say, contemptuous relationship. And here you are now benefiting from her demise. Some would find that not only fortuitous but macabre, wouldn't you say?"

"I wouldn't say. But yes, Marjorie and I were fellow pianists. And in the tightly contested field of music, some could call us rivals. But from my point of view, we shared a healthy, competitive relationship. I'm grief stricken that she is no longer with us, but the symphony's organization called me and asked if I would be so inclined to honor the remaining performances already scheduled. We all have to eat, Mr. Rivers. And I resent the implication that I'm taking advantage of her absence or that I had anything to do with her demise."

"I'm not implying anything, Miss Crane. And I find it curious that you think I am," answered Jake.

After looking chastised and feeling abused, Melissa reached for the interior doors to the complex, claiming:

"If you'll excuse me, I need to go," then hastily, if not anxiously, departed.

Jake's sixth sense was on high alert as he put away, into his breast pocket, the remainder of his business cards.

In the basement rehearsal hall of the Meyerhoff, Anton Rinaldi was keeping at bay the over 100 musicians gathered for the morning's run-through of his Rapsody in C. Not too 'put-out' were they, over the tardy nature of their solo pianist, because unionized musicians get paid by the half hour whether they play or not. Thundering into their midst, breaking their revery, came Melissa Crane with her face all reddened and her lungs out of breath. After smashing her music onto the piano, she beckoned the conductor for a private moment in the hallway outside.

After dejectedly relinquishing his baton to the music stand, Anton joined her in the hallway.

"Do you know what just happened to me?" she hurled in Anton's general direction, which had him retreating from her spittle.

"I haven't the foggiest," he admitted, looking at most, nonplussed.

"A private investigator just waylaid me upstairs in the hallway and practically accused me of murdering Marjorie."

"That's it?" he asked.

"That's it???" she decried.

Anton then turned around and headed back into the rehearsal hall with a fuming Melissa right on his heels. He walked up onto his platform, picked up his baton, and after giving a side-glance to Melissa, who had unceremoniously deposited her derriere onto the piano's bench, announced:

"Enough time has been waisted already with delays and hysterical nonsense. From the top."

He then raised his baton and waited for the orchestra's appropriate response.

Chapter 12

‖:Repeat:‖

Not at all unexpected, Anton was the last to leave the building after that morning's rehearsal. He hesitated in the lobby's vestibule and looked around as if expecting to see someone. After assuring himself that he was quite alone, he proceeded to make his way off the Meyerhoff's grounds to enter the parking lot across the street. One perk about being the last to leave was assuring yourself a quiet and undisturbed few minutes in the restroom. The second was being able to find your car on the lot after everyone else had departed. It was therefore hard for him to miss the tall individual parked 'half-assed' on the hood of his car.

"Don't tell me, let me guess. You want to talk about Marjorie," asked Anton of the stranger.

"No, actually. I want _you_ to talk about Marjorie," answered the tall man.

"Jake Rivers, private investigator," claimed the stranger, handing him one of his business cards.

"Same man who talked to Melissa earlier in the day?" asked Anton.

"The one and only," admitted Jake.

"And what can I tell you that she couldn't?"

"You mean wouldn't," stated Jake.

"Whatever," claimed Anton, as he attempted to unlock his driver's door.

Jake slid off the hood and placed his back's entire weight on the door preventing it from opening.

"Do you want to tell me why you hired, then fired, then rehired Marjorie, only to replace her initially, then finally with Melissa?" asked Jake.

"Really?" chided Anton, not only over the question, but over the fact that Jake was preventing him from leaving.

"Really!" insisted Jake.

"I don't know how it is in your profession," Anton stated in a snidely manner, "but in the professional world of music, there are a lot of narcissistic egotistical prima donnas out there."

"Spoken from personal experience?" insinuated Jake.

Anton ignored the gibe.

"Not to say Marjorie was one of them, mind you, I'm just saying. Sometimes these entities collide and their talents coalesce, allowing the music to win. Sometimes their vehement, shitty personalities clash, and the situation deteriorates into chaos. The result usually isn't pretty."

"Is that what happened?" asked Jake.

Without answering the question asked, Anton continued.

"Marjorie was one of, if not the greatest interpretive pianist I've ever known. I'll miss her terribly. But if you're insinuating that I had anything to do with her death, in order to replace her with Melissa, I'll sue you until your children won't remember you."

Jake came up off the car so fast it startled the shit out of Anton. Intimidating him even more than Jake's nearness and size, was the sheer and unwavering look of feral hatred staring him in the face.

As the look of impending death slowly faded and was replaced by a small smirk, Jake brushed off non-existing lint from Anton's coat, as he claimed:

"I'd be careful, if I were you, writing checks, or in this case, making threats that your ass can't cash."

Not breaking eye contact whatsoever, Jake sidestepped, and then slowly backed away from Anton, who looked as if he was going to faint any minute, until, hoping that he would, but convinced that he wasn't, Jake turned to make his way home, confident that his threat had found its mark.

Meanwhile, inside the Meyerhoff's main hall, high in the air next to the ceiling, Eli Cassilly was stripping wood veneer-patterned contact paper off the surface of previously installed silver foil, that covered the 10-foot circular sound reflecting discs. He subsequently removed the silver foil, exposing the natural, spruce wood construction of the disc itself

"Doctor Cassilly, I presume," echoed off the ceiling after being spoken by a mountain-of-a-man being lifted into the air by a borrowed forklift.

"What-in-the-hell are you doing up here?" screamed Cassilly, after being scared half to death and nearly falling off the platform he was lying on.

Before Murph could respond, he had to shake his head in bewilderment. The more intelligent these 'muckety-mucks' were supposed to be, the dumber they got. He was expecting a better literary response from a 'doctor,' to his obviously famous English literature pronouncement then he received just now.

"Are you, or are you not Doctor Eli Cassilly? It's a simple question, take your time."

Caught between surprise and indignation, Cassilly responded, "Yes, I am."

"Excellent," Murph admitted. "You just saved us a lot of wasted breath."

"Who are you?" asked Cassilly.

"Now we're getting somewhere. Direct questions. I like that," stated Murph, as he pulled out a business card and handed it to the good doctor.

"Patrick Murphy, private investigator," he declared.

"So, what are you doing up here, Doc?"

Cassilly was confused as to why a PI would be up here talking to him. He was torn between righteous indignation, therefore blowing this guy off, and basic human curiosity.

"If I told you, you wouldn't understand," claimed Cassilly.

"You'd be surprised at what I'm capable of understanding, Doc. Try me."

Not knowing just why he was doing so, Cassilly began to explain to Murph his theories of sound reflection and how it pertained to the theater going public's greater appreciation of music.

The doctor was right. Murph didn't comprehend half of what Cassilly was explaining to him. All he wanted to do was to keep him talking, so that the pocket voice recorder he had enabled, prior to entering his current lofty position, recorded every word of explanation coming out of Cassilly's mouth. Murph figured he'd have plenty of time to analyze what Cassilly was preaching, later, over a dram of the 'good-stuff.' He was also maneuvering himself into position to subvertly capture, on digital film, via smartphone, a picture of what the doc was doing.

After realizing that he had gleaned what was pertinent, and that the doctor was just enjoying listening to his own voice, Murph interrupted his prattling by asking:

"And you knew Marjorie Cunningham, right?"

This pronouncement brought the blathering to a screeching halt.

"Why, yes. Yes, I did," he answered in a confused manner.

"You guys had a pretty good rift going on over your, 'so-called' tuning of the hall. Not once, but on numerous occasions as I understand. In fact, every time she played here, right?"

The doctor didn't need the building to fall on his head in order to realize why this man was here and where this line of questioning was headed.

"Does the manager of the theater know that you're up here?" asked the doctor, trying to divert the nature of the questions being asked.

"Absolutely. They told me exactly where to find you," chuckled Murph. "Now, answer the question," he insisted.

Cassilly hesitated momentarily before saying, "Yes, that's true, we did have our differences of opinion over the proper and most judicious way the hall could/should be tuned. Why? Where is all this heading? The poor unfortunate woman is dead. How does whether or not we agreed upon 'hall tuning' have anything to do with, ---anything?" inquired Cassilly.

"Just asking, Doc. For the record, just asking," was heard fading away, as Murph, with all sought-after information literally in hand, slowly descended to the floor of the concert hall, leaving Cassilly 'dry-and-high.'

On his way out of the hall, Murph first heard, then spotted a familiar 'face', elbows deep, bent over a grand piano, center stage.

"That wouldn't be the one and only Jonah Pyke now, would it?" Murph teased, as he approached the technician hard at work.

"Oh, hey there Mr. Murphy. What brings you here?" asked Jonah, as he sat on the pianos' bench, looking forlorn, pretending he couldn't guess. Since meeting Claire Adams the day Marjorie Cunningham died, he and Claire have shared a few luncheon dates and got to know each other, and the subject at hand, a little better.

"Collecting information from people in the know," answered Murph.

"And how's that going?" asked Jonah, sincerely interested in the answer.

"As might be expected. A tid bit here, a tad there," replied Murph.

"How about you?" Murph asked.

Jonah looked down at his lap, where he was absentmindedly twirling his tuning wrench in his hand as he replied:

"Quiet, Mr. Murphy. Eerily quiet. Miss Cunningham used to meet me here on the stage every day prior to her performances to help me tune the piano. Well, she really didn't do anything to physically help me 'tune' the piano, I think she was giving me moral support more than anything. I really miss that. When we first met, we didn't hit-it-off so well. But while getting to know her, I came to appreciate my profession better, through her eyes. Or, maybe I should say, through her ears."

Jonah stopped there just then and took on the mantle of one that was reliving a moment from the past that only he could see. When he looked up, he realized that Murph was anxiously waiting for him to finish his story.

"Don't get me wrong," he chuckled, "she was always a stickler for detail. Everything had to be just so. But after she got her hearing aids, she was even more so. The enhancement to her hearing seemed to give her a greater appreciation for sounds' subtleties. She was so vain. She didn't want anyone to know she was wearing them. And they didn't, after she started to wear her hair long again. But I found out one day by chance. While we were both noses deep over the strings, I accidentally dropped my tuning wrench directly onto the harp of the piano, and she grabbed the side of her head and winced. When I asked her what was wrong, she had to 'fess-up' about wearing the assistive devices. ---- She sure could play this piano," he admitted, as his tear-filled eyes slowly gazed upon the instrument, whose music only he could hear.

Murph could empathize with Jonah over the loss of a friend. During Jonah's 'walk-down-memory-lane,' the face of Doris,

Jake's previous secretary, filled Murph's vision; her laughter filled his ears, and the weight of her inert body, as he carried her from out of the basement where she was murdered, could be felt upon his arms, even now.

The two men, unaware that they had just shared a related experience, appreciated the few seconds of silence that connected them thereafter. Or, upon reflection, maybe they did after all.

Chapter 13

1st Ending:

"He was here all-day asking questions."

"And what did you tell him?"

"I didn't tell him anything."

"Are you sure?"

"Sure, I'm sure. What do you take me for?"

"Hopefully, not a fool."

That comment didn't go over well, as could be deduced from the silence on the other end of the phone.

"Let's make sure 'nothing' is all the information he ever receives."

There wasn't the need for a response, because there was no one on the phone any longer to hear it.

Chapter 14

Requiem for a Pianist

As much as the music critics tried to paint a rosy picture of Rinaldi's Rhapsody with Melissa Crane at the piano, they couldn't help but compare the results against the Rhapsody's opening night performance with Marjorie Cunningham, albeit tragic and short lived. And they published as much in all the trade magazines. The Meyerhoff's ticket office saw only a brief surge in ticket sales, status post the tragedy that befell its hallowed halls on opening night. Many pundits attributed this to curiosity seekers for one, and music critics, eager to cite the differences for another. Since then, attendance has been tepid, at best.

The medical examiner, after exhausting all known possibilities, finally came to the conclusion that Marjorie Cunningham's death was not from natural causes, and therefore officially pronounced her death a homicide. This laid to rest all doubts on the subject from a medical, and now subsequent judicial aspect.

Today, the Meyerhoff's facade was adorned with huge black banners signifying mourning, as it laid to rest one of its own. The board of trustees had approached Claire, Marjorie's only living relative, and asked if formal ceremonies for Marjorie could be held on its main stage, with tributes to her throughout the building. Claire couldn't imagine a more befitting place for her aunt to be eulogized, so she readily accepted their offer.

Subdued string quartets, muffled pianos and beleaguered instrumentalists could be seen and heard paying musical tributes to their fallen comrade in every hallway and vestibule throughout the building. Pictures of Marjorie in every phase of physical, as well as professional development, could be seen, poster-sized, hanging everywhere. Flowers of every variety, in all colors and forms of arrangements adorned the hallways, balconies, and lined the aisles leading to the stage, upon which sat a coffin. And not just any coffin. One specifically designed to look like a piano, with flowers, depicting the ivory and ebony colors of the keys, sprayed out and overflowed the stage to the floor below. Fans, relatives, and professional musical colleagues alike, roamed the byways comparing shared memories, or sat in silent communion throughout the hall.

Among the silent communicants, seated midway up section 'A,' was Jake Rivers and his family, as well as those associated with his business. Also present among them was Claire Adams, accompanied by Jonah Pyke. The main topic of conversation, presently, seemed to be the recent news circulating from the ME's office. Jake passed out the official report to everyone in attendance. While Bach's Mass in B minor (BWV 232) was being played as background music by the chamber orchestra seated on stage behind the catafalque, the conversations in section 'A' continued.

"But just because the police are now involved doesn't mean you're going to stop your own investigations, does it, Mr. Rivers? " asked a concerned Claire.

"A promise is a promise," confirmed Jake, as he sealed the deal once again with a firm handshake.

As everyone settled back to listen to the conclusion of Bach's Mass, Michael Lamm, Colonel of the military's national guards' fighter jet wing, stationed at Martins airfield in middle river, after silently, but thoroughly 'digesting' the ME's report, leaned forward in his seat, and in Jake's ear whispered,

"I need to talk to you, today, at the office, after the ceremonies."

Jake just nodded his head in affirmation.

Murph, after lowering his head to be privy himself to Micheal's pronouncement, spied a piece of silver foil on the floor next to his seat. Resembling the inside packaging of a pack of cigarettes, but knowing that it wasn't, Murph bent over and retrieved it off the floor. And, as the solo bagpiper from far aloft in the balcony played 'Amazing Grace,' guiding Marjorie's soul heavenward, Murph guided the newly acquired piece of foil securely into his breast pocket.

Most, but not all mourners were transfixed on the soloist. Some were taking particular notice of the conclave transpiring in section 'A'.

JAKE
RIVERS
&
ASSOCIATE
PRIVATE
INVESTIGATIVE
SERVICES

Chapter 15

On the Homefront

After ceremonies for Marjorie had taken place all day long at the Meyerhoff, a brief, but poignant tribute was performed graveside, as they laid her to rest. Jake Rivers, et al., from section 'A', were invited to attend a private gathering at Jake Rivers and Associate's office, located in downtown Baltimore, after all the formal ceremonies had concluded for the day. The Rivers', especially Bridget, had volunteered their space and time to help Claire, as a single individual, coordinate food and drinks for everyone, knowing that Claire probably didn't have the time, nor the energy, to do so herself.

Among the many 'high points' of the day, in juxtaposition to the low ones, was watching Clair and Jonah's reaction to being introduced to Babe. Dumfounded, then awestruck was an understatement. As the two humans were being formally introduced to everyone's favorite reptile, Michael Lamm had made his way over to where Jake was conversing with Murph and beckoned them, clandestinely, to join him in the corner of Jake's office. There, they were met by Catherine (Murphy) Lamm, former Captain of the Marine Corps.

"I wanted to broach this subject with the two of you after reading the ME's report concerning Marjorie Cunningham."

He took a moment just then to glance at his wife, who, obviously privy to what Michael was going to divulge, gave her head a nod, indicating to him that he should continue.

"What I'm going to tell you isn't common knowledge, outside of the military, so I ask that discretion be the better part of valor."

Needless to say, he now had Jake and Murph's full attention.

"Do the two of you remember back in 2016, our embassy's staff in Cuba had a malady running rampant through its ranks that nobody could figure out?"

"Isn't that where everybody was getting sick and nauseous and nobody knew why?" asked Murph.

"Exactly," claimed Michael. "Back then we called it the 'Havana Syndrome.' It began with the diplomats in Havana hearing strange sounds and feeling intense cranial pressure, resulting in severe headaches, increased blood pressure, dizziness, tinnitus, hearing loss, balance problems, memory issues and cognitive fog. Investigators at the time cited the most probable cause as being pulsed radio frequencies in the form of microwave energy. The military picked up on this hypothesis and ran with it, and they've invested countless manhours ever since studying and perfecting this weapon."

"Weapon?" asked Jake.

"Weapon," reassured Michael.

"The military complex up at Aberdeen Proving Ground in north-east Maryland not only makes and tests armaments, chemical and biological weaponry, but has been the country's research and developmental testing site for Electronic Warfare (EW). Intelligent Electronic Warfare and Sensors (IEW+S) along with Cyber Signals Intelligence (SIGINT) has been conducting combat field tests for over ten years. They've developed technology on a broad scale, right down to handheld battlefield equipment that, when 'tuned' to the right electromagnetic waves, could give enemy combatants instantaneous headaches and diarrhea, to melting their organs where they once stood. Believe me, these weapons exist. I've seen these weapons in action, personally."

He then picked up the ME's report and held it out in front of him as one would a testimonial.

"And this looks damn close."

Jake and Murph could only stare at Michael and Katie, who, by the look on both their faces, were dead-serious.

"But that was on a massive, global scale. Having it affect a single individual, if that is what this is altogether, is quite different," stated Michael.

"And you know of no one else in the building that night that was affected in any way similar to Marjorie, or, for that matter, at all?" asked Katie.

"No, no one. At least not that we know of," claimed Jake.

Jake then indicated to Michael and Katie that involving Bridget and Claire, both emergency room RNs at the University of Maryland's shock trauma unit, would not only be prudent, but necessary. After calling them over to participate in their discussions, Jake asked the pair:

"The night Marjorie died, or even in the days that followed, to your knowledge, did the hospital, or anywhere else for that matter, report any patients complaining of increased head pressure, elevated blood pressure, dizziness, tinnitus, hearing loss or balance problems."

"Is that all?" Bridget flippantly remarked, until she realized that those asking the questions were serious. Bridget then looked to Claire for collaboration, when she replied in earnest, "No, not that I recall. As a matter of fact, the staff had remarked at the end of the week, as to how relatively 'medically' quiet the week had been."

She received a reaffirming head nod of confirmation from Claire. This statement, apparently, was not what the four congregants expected to hear.

"OK, following up and pursuing your line of thinking, what would be our next step?" asked Murph.

"Pursuing what line of thinking?" asked Claire.

Michael and Katie, along with Jake and Murph, now explained to Bridget and Claire what they had been previously discussing and their current hypothesis on the matter.

Just afterward, Jake reached out and grabbed the coroner's report from Michael, stating,

"The ME's ex-military. He's bound to have been exposed and privy to this type of experimentation, as you claim has been taking place over the years. I think our next plan of action should be to pay a visit to the good doctor.

Chapter 16

ppp

(Pianississimo)

Entering a morgue, no matter who you are, always causes you to become exceptionally quiet. Even though the morgue itself is naturally exceptionally quiet. Maybe it's our way of honoring the dead and showing them respect. Because they're quiet and still, presumably we must be also? If one were to make an overt, obnoxious sound, no one within would be the wiser, except the living working there, who could hear it. So why then would we be quiet for the living?

It's even harder for a gaggle of people, hell bent on seeing the coroner, to muffle the sounds of their approaching feet or silence their jabbering lips.

When Murph informed the ME that he/they would be paying him a visit in the a.m., he wasn't quite prepared for the onslaught. He had to say, however, that not only was he pleased by the interruption in his day but was glad to see those who had interrupted him. After warmly greeting Murph, followed by Jake, both of whom he knew well, the ME was treated to the introductions of Colonel Michael Lamm of the Air National Guard and Lieutenant Catherine Lamm of the Maryland State Police and EMT helicopter pilot for the U of MD Emergency Medical Systems. And herself, formally

Captain Murphy of the Marines. Accompanying them were Bridget McCall RN, whose husband, Tony, he knew all too well, and Claire Adams, who unfortunately, he had the pleasure of meeting several weeks ago.

"Please, do come in and have a seat," he requested of one and all, after formal introductions had concluded.

"And what do I owe the pleasure of such an illustrious collection of the living," jovially asked the ME.

"You know we're investigating the death of Marjorie Cunningham," Murph exclaimed by way of explanation.

"Yes, I'm well aware of that," he said in response. He then turned his attention to Claire, stating, "Once again, I'm sorry for your loss, and I'm doubly sorry for having to miss her eulogy. I heard it was very, -- moving,"

"Thank you, Doctor, and yes, it was," confirmed Claire.

"What do you know about the 'Havana Syndrome,'" interjected Jake, as if it were the next logical sentence following Claire's, "Yes, it was."

Slightly confused by the strange segue, but knowing his company the way he did, and fathoming they had a very good reason for the request, it was not completely ---unexpected.

"Yes, I'm quite familiar with that malady. In fact, I treated several diplomats from that embassy when they were flown back to the US." As he spoke, he gestured to the wall behind where he sat, to point out diplomas and certificates. One in particular, designating him as a retired major in the army and credentialed as a member of the Armed Forces Medical Examiner System (AFMES).

"And how about Aberdeen Proving Ground's work on Electronic Warfare," asked Murph in rapid succession.

It was now the doctor's turn to honor the dead as he remained stoically silent.

"It's OK, Doc," claimed Michael, as he showed the ME his badge and credentials listing all the right, 'special clearance' acronyms needed, that the ME recognized all-to-well from his own military experiences, allowing him to speak. "I've already filled them in on the subject."

The ME appeared as though a large weight had been removed from his tongue, when he replied,

"I'm very well versed on the subject. Why?" replied the ME.

"Because to my eyes, the etiology and symptoms displayed by the victims of intense microwave radiation, like those in Cuba, and those irradiated by our," --- and he hesitated here before continuing, "our electromagnetic technology, appear eerily similar to that which killed Marjorie Cunningham."

The ME slowly reclined in his chair and raised his right hand to cover his lips. Then his face took on the far away expression of deep thought. After several contemplative moments, the ME, addressing Michael directly said,

"I can see where you're coming from and why you would think that. Similar yes, but the same, no. In the one case, it's global, broad spectrum general maladies, affecting multiple systems simultaneously and in general, not lethal. In the other, it's very specific and accurate; unidirectional and targeted, and deadly.

"But, -- could it be done?" asked Michael.

Once again, the doctor took on that far-away look and returned to his former 'thinking posture.'

After he took a longer time contemplating Michael's question, the doctor answered by saying, "Yes, I believe it could be done. But it would be involved."

"How so?" asked Katie.

"Since we're talking about a single individual here, that person would need to be outfitted, equipped with a receiver that had microchip hardware, specifically designed to utilize software modulators and oscillators tuned specifically and unnaturally for them. Then bombarded by envelope generating amplifiers so intense as to simultaneously rupture every blood vessel in that person's head."

Claire stood up then, quite suddenly, and after reaching into her pocketbook, withdrew her hand, producing her aunt's hearing aids and smartphone.

"You mean, like these?"

Needless to say, everyone in the room sat transfixed. The doctor slowly extended his palm, requesting the items which Claire lovingly deposited into his outstretched hand.

"Where, where did you . . .?"

"You presented them to me after your autopsy. They're the only tangible items that my aunt possessed, besides her clothes, her music, and her piano."

The other members of the entourage slowly stood to gape at the proffered belongings, as if by doing so, they could see more clearly the objects in question, as well as the solution to the mystery.

The ME directed his anticipatory gaze to each in turn, then finally trained his attention on Michael Lamm.

"I still have connections with trusted personnel up at Aberdeen. If I could get these to them, . . . "

"Consider it done," claimed Michael, as he reached into his pocket, withdrew his smartphone and began to dial.

As the ME continued to be mesmerized by what he held in his hand, Murph slowly advanced on where the ME was sitting, and from within the pocket of his coat withdrew a roughly 5"x 5" piece of silver foil, then presented it to the doctor, saying:

"You might want to have them take a look at this while they're at it."

Chapter 17

Rubato

"If these walls could talk"

Most music aficionados, when asked to describe a Symphony Hall, would most likely talk about its spacious interior, style of decor and marvelous acoustical design built into the very fabric of its architecture. But most of all, the inspirational and moving music it conveyed to its audience time and time again. What no one would speak of, because they probably never had the experience, outside of when they were present for a concert, naturally, would be to be on site, to appreciate its silence, when empty.

The most profound silences one could experience in this world, just ask the lonely, could be provided by a morgue, a church and graveyard at night, or a Concert Hall when not in use. Walking through the empty basement corridors, or for that matter, the hall itself, during times without a concert, could be tantamount to one of the quietest and loneliest experiences a human being could ever have during their lifetime. Just ask those who worked there, or in this case, one piano tuner on his way to the nearest restroom.

The silence surrounding him was so profound, he could hear his own heart beating. That being so, Jonah Pyke could not help but hear the heightened argument, taking place not 30 feet away, coming from the office of the hall's music director, Anton Rinaldi, between him, and the pianist Melissa Crane. He usually wasn't one to eavesdrop, but as he crept along the hallway, not wanting to be discovered, but in dire need of the facility not 20 feet away, he couldn't help but overhear. He ducked into the restroom just in time not to embarrass himself. Even from his newly found vantage point, although muffled, he could still hear what they were saying. Realizing, if <u>he</u> could hear them, <u>they</u> could hear him, he elected not to flush the toilet or use the sink to wash his hands, thus giving himself away, because the information he had gleaned while relieving himself needed to get to the authorities ASAP, and he personally knew just where to go.

Jake and Murph, nestled in their office on Calvert Street, were waiting to hear back from the scientific military experts at Aberdeen, by way of the ME in Baltimore, the results of the tests on Marjorie Cunningham's hearing aids and smartphone. Who they weren't waiting for, or didn't expect to hear from, was Jonah Pyke as he bulldozed his way into their office shouting about "something important."

Jake didn't have to tell Marguerite, his secretary, to 'send him back' to his office, because Jonah was already there.
Murph followed the whirlwind that was Jonah into Jake's office, from his own, via sheer atmospheric disturbance.

"Slow up, slow up," Jake instructed. "I know you have something to say, but at the rate you're going, you're going to give yourself an attack."

Red in the face, and panting extremely fast, Jonah accepted Jake's advice, as well as the chair Jake presented to him, and sat down. Murph did likewise without so much as a 'make-yourself-comfortable-as-well,' from Jake.
Marguerite, in true Marguerite fashion, had a glass of water at Jonah's elbow before his tush even touched the chair. She then sat down in the chair opposite Murph; all without saying. After several moments of rest, as well as several sips of the water, Jonah went on to explain to Jake Rivers and Associate, et al., what he remembered of the conversation that he overheard.

"Rinaldi was pretty pissed," claimed Jonah. "He was real upset that Marjorie was dead."

"We're all upset that she's dead," admitted Marguerite.

"Yes, I know, but not like that. I got the distinct impression that he was upset 'because' she was dead. At one time, Mellissa said to him, *"What did you think she was going to do, stop arguing with you over interpretive ideas? Or stop playing the piano altogether and just move over, simply to let me in?"*

"Then she went on to say, *"You just make sure you take me with you on any piano based concerts, and I'll make sure you get your check.""*

"That sure does sound like something that should be looked into," admitted Jake.

"I'm on it," claimed Murph.

"Do you think we should tell Claire?" asked Jonah, as he took another sip of water, while the members of Jake Rivers and Associate stifled a grin.

"Let's wait to see what Murph turns up. I like to keep this type of information 'close-to-home' for now, if you know what I mean," stated Jake, as he held his index finger up beside his nose.

Jonah nodded his head in affirmation, understanding all too well the need for restraint and anonymity, but having no real clue what Jake meant by that gesture. The only other time in his life he ever saw that being used was by a picture of Santa Clause, in an illustrated version of:

'The Night before Christmas.'

Chapter 18

Decelerando Decrescendo

As Murph was rummaging through bank records of four specific individuals, whose court orders for same were legally obtained, the members of the military's scientific community at Aberdeen Proving Ground were unwrapping a parcel from a well-known medical colleague of theirs, who used to be one of them: hand delivered by the commanding officer of Maryland's Air National Guard no-less. Going without saying, the package was given top priority.

Established in 1917, to meet the country's obligations concerning its recently declared war against the Central Powers, Aberdeen began its assistance to the nation as a war munition's testing facility. It remains today the U.S. army's premier center for research, development, testing, and evaluation (RDT & E) of military technology, covering everything from weapons and vehicles to communications, cyber, and chemical defense. So, it was with some surprise for the scientists to see a package, addressed as 'PRIORITY 1,' come into their midst from the medical examiner of Baltimore. Even more surprising was the contents of said package. Along with the contents came a note, which read:

"Who-Ah from an old colleague. But don't hold that against me. I urgently need your help. Put the best electromagnetic and audio specialists on this. Can't tell you more for confidentiality reasons. Don't want to bias your findings either. Justice rests on your analysis. ASAP please."

*Major (retired) Jonathan Burke MD, PhD, ME, **AFMES.***

The items were distributed as asked, and to the appropriate/applicable personnel, as asked, in a manner befitting the military's slogan: with "All asses and elbows."

It didn't take the specialists long to locate the abnormalities that lay therein and to speculate on their function.

And in true military medical fashion, they relayed their findings to the ME, STAT. No sooner did the ME read their report than he communicated their findings, along with his summation, to Jake Rivers and Associate, as well as Sgt. Pamela Richardson, Homicide Detective, BCPD.

Chapter 19

Coda

Subsequent to the findings of the military's electronic warfare specialists concerning Marjorie Cunningham's hearing aids and smartphone, along with their analysis of the reflective material found on the convex discs of the Meyerhoff; bank account information discovered by Murph, coupled with the verbal testimony of Jonah Pyke and Clair Adams, warrants for the arrest of Anton Rinaldi, Mellissa Crane, Eli Cassilly and Felice Hoeman were issued. In due course, the subjects were found, arrested and imprisoned, where they are currently waiting to stand trial for the murder of Marjorie Cunningham.

Upon reading about the arrests, Jonah Pyke informed Claire Adams, who together, were presently en route to the home of Jake and Nina Rivers, where a small dinner gathering was about to celebrate well deserved sleuthing. And by small was meant the entire Rivers clan. On the menu: stuffed pork chops, naturally.

Once there, they were cordially treated to introductions by everyone assembled, and introduced to, the 'good-stuff.' Following multiple, and diverse discussions taking place everywhere, about literally everything from everybody, dinner was served.

"Mrs. Rivers, that was the best stuffed porkchops I've ever tasted," said Jonah, after having three servings himself. The thunderous cacophony which followed, off the beating of crystalware from everyone around the table, affirmed Jonah's statement.

"Couldn't have said it better myself," claimed Murph.

"And you have," echoed Jake.

As the after-dinner wine was being poured, Jonah looked toward the head of the table, where Jake sat, and claimed, "I still can't wrap my head around the intricacies of this case; when I do, I start to get a headache."

Chuckles from more than one person could be heard making their way around the table.

"Join the crowd," came the retort from an unknown source.

Jake, recognizing a cue to speak when he heard one, lifted his newly poured drink and leaned back into his chair. Recognizing a 'story-to-come,' everyone else did the same.

"Marjorie Cunningham was not only talented, but opinionated," he began. This apparent 'statement-of-fact' was met with 'cat calls' from the females and grunts from the males.

"Hey, if anyone else wants to do this, be my guest," Jake advised, looking pseudo-sternly around the table.
Conceding defeat, basically because no one else could or even wanted to take on the story's mantle, everyone relented.

"And that will be the last interruption for the night," berated Jake, as only the loving head of the household could. Settling back into his chair, again, he began; again.

"As I was saying, before I was rudely interrupted," and he gazed around the table to make sure that this time he wasn't going to be, then continued: "Marjorie Cunningham was not only talented, but opinionated. And in her flamboyant, professional style, she rubbed some people the wrong way. She outperformed a rival pianist, Melissa Crane, in her own profession, she embarrassed a music director, Anton Rinaldi, by showing him that her interpretive skills were better than his, even on his own creation, and she called to task the incompetence of a doctor of acoustic engineering, Eli Cassilly.

All for the love of music. That's what was just taking place on the surface. Behind the scenes, you had Felice Hoeman, an audiologist who had formulated and utilized a theory for sound manipulation that was benefiting many in multiple fields. She'd written about it and put it into practice. Then along comes a man, a doctor in acoustic engineering, who steals her invention, modifies it, and then exploits it for his own gain. The scientific field gives him credit for it and she is widely forgotten. Along comes a rival pianist who knows about the contention between Marjorie Cunningham and the music director, Anton Rinaldi. She also knows about the animosity between her and Eli Cassilly. What she doesn't know, until she meets Felice Hoeman, is that Felice is Eli Cassilly's niece. Then she also finds out about the professional and academic rift between Felice and her uncle. But it's not until she discovers that Marjorie is losing her hearing and that Felice is her audiologist does her little plot begin to take shape.

According to bank records of the people in question, that were obtained, and have now been turned over to the prosecutors, the following theories have emerged.

Melissa convinces Rinaldi that if Marjorie's 'out-of-the-picture,' she could take her place. And, in doing so, promises Rinaldi a cut of her earnings every time she accompanies him. She convinces Felice that she should extort her uncle's use of her ideas, which, by the way, she has patents for, so as to ruin his reputation and discredit him in the scientific community if he doesn't 'play along.'. So now Felice is receiving payments from Melissa, who is endorsing her entrainment theory during music therapy sessions, which Felice herself is sponsoring, as well as receiving 'contributions' from her uncle's endeavors tuning concert halls. Knowing that Felice is Marjorie's audiologist, Melissa has Felice threaten her uncle again with exposure if he doesn't modify his 'techniques,' i.e., to bastardize and manipulate sound in a prescribed, detrimental capacity of her making. She then has Felice modify Margorie's cellphone and hearing aids so that Marjorie would literally kill herself while she played."

"And how in the world did she do that?" asked Jonah.

"She knew of the Rhapsody being written by Rinaldi, in what key he meant to write it, and his choice of pianist to perform it. She knew that Rinaldi was using the propensity and proprietary use of the tonal frequency of "C" throughout the piece. She had Felice modify receivers in the hearing aids and the amplifiers in the cellphone to not only be oversensitive to the pitch frequencies but also the harmonics of "C", i.e., that being 261.63 Hz, that's middle C (C4); 523.25 Hz, C5, it's octave; 1046.50 Hz, C6, it's octave, and exponentially onward. The phone, along with its micro-components in the hearing aids, and with specifically written software not only enhanced those frequencies, but they also elevated, then sustained them to where the accumulative effect, as Marjorie played, therefore stimulating her own natural biological entrainment, reverberated the inside of her vessels so rhythmically and precisely, that they exploded. Accentuating and focusing all this energy, was the silver foil Eli Cassilly had fashioned over the hall's reflective baffles. The specific composition of the foil was hypersensitive to the tonal frequency of "C." Similar to the way certain thicknesses of glass reverberate to certain noises (frequencies) from the outside world causing them to rattle, or objects in your home, bounce across the table's countertop, when a certain passage of music is played on your stereo.

The foil reverberated to, then radiated frequencies of "C" throughout the hall, which was picked up and modified by Marjorie's cellphone. The more she played . . . ,"

"The faster she died," concluded Claire, who then wiped a single tear from her cheek.

"That's why no one else in the hall was affected but her," stated Jonah, finally comprehending the complex and extraordinary means by which jealousy and hatred could drive people.

"But Rinaldi didn't do anything to my aunt but dislike and envy her," stated Claire. "Why was he arrested?"

"Directly, no," answered Murph. "But he may have to prove that he wasn't an accessory to the crime. After all, he did indirectly benefit from her death. Besides, that's what trials are all about. Hey, did I ever tell you about the time Jake found me all beaten up in the basement of a convenience store?"

As Murph began to elaborate, some guests at the table poured more wine, others simply excused themselves. Jake stayed, because Claire and Jonah stayed. Besides, somebody had to

interject the truth into the story now and again, just to keep
the record straight.

Reprise

-- 6 months later –

Time: 8 am
Location: Meyerhoff Symphony Hall
Purpose: Tuning the piano for tonight's Beethoven piano
concerto #5 in E-flat Major, Op. 73

Performer: Eugene Eckhart

Because the Symphony's Hall was as quiet as a tomb, it was hard to miss the tinkering sounds and constant tuning and retuning of piano strings echoing throughout. Elbows deep inside the harp strings of the Steinway, centrally located on the Meyerhoff's main stage was the well-recognized 'face' (derriere) of Jonah Pike, the Meyerhoff's preferred piano technician.

"Achem!" came the coughing sound from the first row. Raising his body and eventually his 'real face' from the belly-of-the-beast, Jonah turned to recognize the all-too-familiar face she always carried with her.

"Hey!" said Claire Adams.

"Hey, right back at 'cha," responded Jonah.

As he started wiping his hands on his utility cloth, in an attempt to clean them, he made his way to the stage's apron in order to help Claire climb up and join him at its edge, where they could sit and talk.

"So, what brings you here?" Jonah asked.

"Oh, I was just in the neighborhood and thought I'd stop by to say, 'hi,'" she lied.

"Oh, that's nice," he stated.

"Yes, yes, it is," she replied, hiding the smirk that was threatening to break free.

"I really stopped by to let you know that I'm going on vacation," she declared.

"Really?" he commented.
"Really," she repeated.

"And when would that be?" he inquired.

"In two weeks," she stated.

"Two weeks?" he parroted.

"Yep, two weeks," she reiterated.

"And pray tell," he began, feeling like he was pulling teeth, "where would this be?" he inquired.

"Vienna, Austria," she claimed.
"Vienna . . . . ., Austria?" he proclaimed, in a truly surprised, dry-mouthed fashion.

He then became very introspective when he softly stated, while looking into his lap:
"Your aunt always wanted to go to Vienna."

The two just sat there in shared silence, before Claire responded, "Yeah, I know. That's why I'm going."

"Beethoven, right?" he said absentmindedly.
"Beethoven, right," she concluded, as she picked up a concert playbill from the stage.

"Beethoven, right?" she inquired, pointing at his picture.
"Yeah, right, Beethoven," he answered, as they both chuckled over the awkward, silly joke.

Jonah continued to nervously clean absolutely nothing off his hands with his rag, as he sat there digesting what she had just declared, and ruminating over its implications.

"How long are you going to be away?" he asked.
"Three weeks," she replied.

"Three weeks, huh," he worried.
"Yep, three entire weeks in Austria," she teased.

Looking downtrodden and not really wanting to hear any more of what she had to say, Jonah decried, "Well, I hope you have a wonderful time on your vacation."

"I would," she claimed, "if I had the right company."

The hands he had been previously 're-cleaning' raw with his towel, suddenly ceased their finagling.

"Would you . . . , would you mind if I tagged along?" he voiced in a stuttering, sincere cadence.

Without answering, she reached into the pocket of her vest and pulled out two pristine airfare tickets to Vienna.

"I hoped you'd ask," she finally admitted, then smiled.

Fine

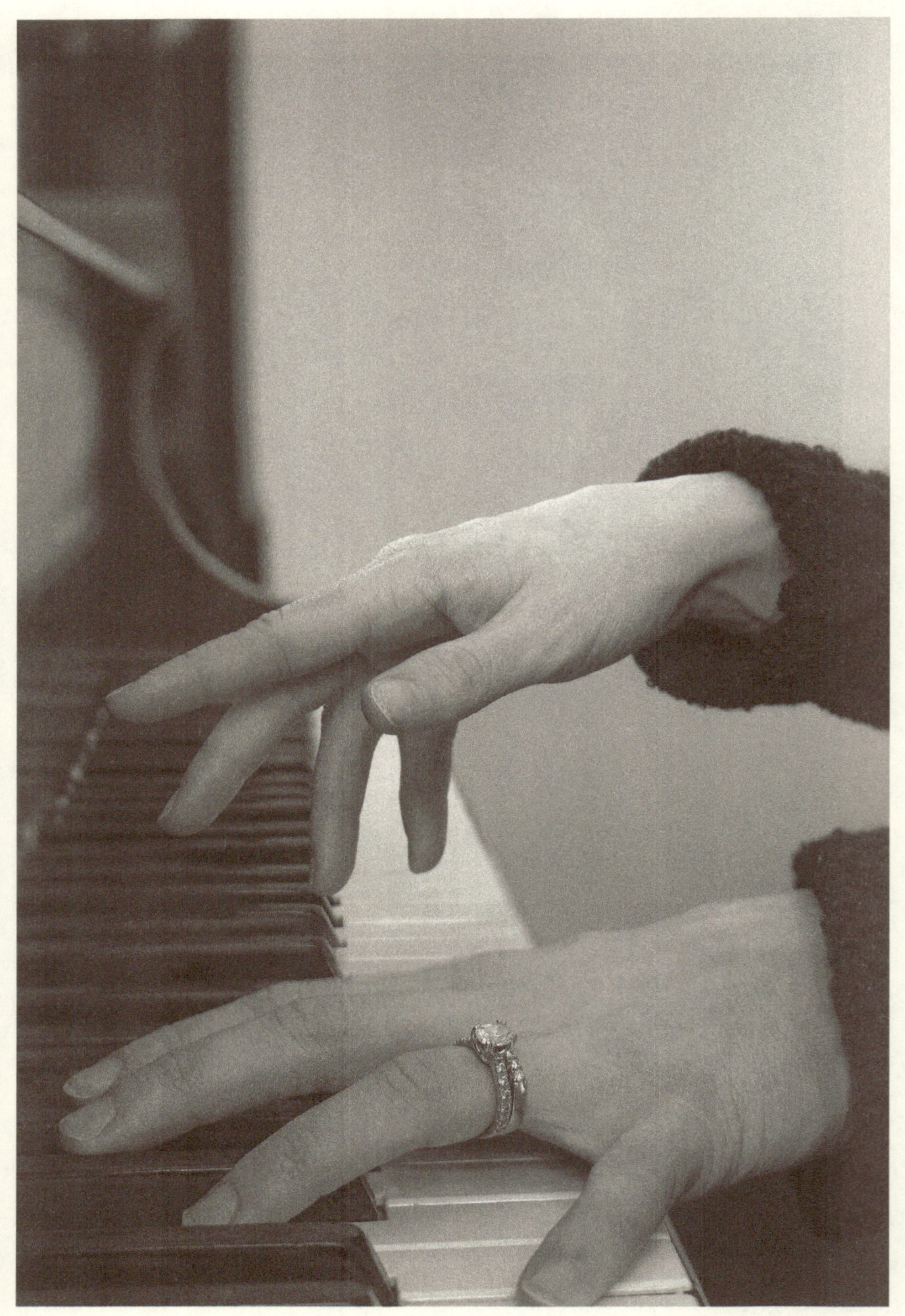

Epilogue

Atypical of any symphony's organization, would be the recording of music from the main stage during a performance or rehearsal, unless specifically contracted by the Board of Trustees to do so, either for themselves and posterity, or promotionally by a third party in advance.

How it came to be, and by whose authority sanctioned it into existence, to this day is unknown. But the final rehearsal of Anton Rinaldi's Rhapsody in C with Marjorie Cunningham at the piano found its way off the stage that day and into the hall's recording studio. When the powers that be discovered it, they had it processed, produced, then released to the public via CD, and in every digital format known to mankind.

It is currently hailed as arguably one of the most renowned and best performed piano Rhapsody's in the world.

Special thanks to the following artists and companies for their contribution of free clip art.

<u>Pixabay</u>
OpenClipart-Vectors
Clker-Free-Vector-Images
Gerd Altmann
Gordan Johnson
WikimediaImages
Wolfgang Eckert
Sunrise
Kailingpiano
Artadder
ChiemSeherin
Pablo Jimenez
Johanna Daher
Holger Schué
Tyli Jura
Vilius Kukanauskas
Moondance
M. Harris
Kalhh
Angela
WikiImages
Oljamu
OurWhisky Foundation

Special thanks to

Doug Byerly

for his editing assistance

Jake Rivers

Adventure Series

About the author…

Joe Mannherz is a Physical Therapist by profession. Retired. He has been singing since the age of 8. From boy soprano in his church choir to tenor in his high school and later college chorus. He also plays several instruments. He's even built his own Vibraphone and Marimbas. He has been a member of the Barbershop Harmony Society for over 45 years; a 30-year member of the Baltimore Symphony Chorus; a member of the Handel Choir and the Concert Artists of Maryland. He has been the Musical Director of Harford County's "Bay Country Gentlemen" and Harrisburg's "Keystone Capital Chorus". He is currently the Artistic/Musical Director of his jazz quintet "High Five" and the "Baltimore Vocal Jazz Ensemble." Along with directing/music arranging/vocal coaching, he can add several stage appearances to his credit; A Funny thing happened on the way to the Forum, 1776, Man of La Mancha, Sound of Music, O'er the Ramparts, Little Mermaid, Jesus Christ Superstar, the Wizard of Oz, and Beauty and the Beast to name a few of the most recent. He is also the author of the fantasy adventures, "The Tale of Jonathan T. Bookworm" and "The Account of Hercules A. Gnawer," both a Plymouth Adventure.